Back to One: Take 4

Slating Magic Hour

By Antonia Gavrihel

Hidden Shelf Publishing House
P.O. Box 4168, McCall, ID 83638
www.hiddenshelfpublishinghouse.com

Slating Magic Hour

Copyright @ 2024, Antonia Gavrihel
Hidden Shelf Publishing House
All rights reserved

Artist: Megan Whitfield

Editor: Robert D. Gaines

Graphic Design: Rachel Wickstrom

Interior Layout: Kerstin Stokes

Library of Congress Cataloguing-in-Publication Data

Name: Gavrihel, Antonia, author.
Title: *Slating Magic Hour* / Antonia Gavrihel.
Series: Back to One
Description: McCall, ID: Hidden Shelf Publishing House, 2024.
Identifiers: ISBN: 978-1-955893-34-3 (paperback) | 978-1-955893-39-8 (epub) | 978-1-955893-40-4 (Kindle)
Subjects: LCSH Motion picture actors and actresses--Fiction. | Celebrities--Fiction. | Marriage--Fiction. | Women--Fiction. | Young Adult --Fiction. | Family--Fiction. | Man-woman relationships--Fiction. | Romance--Fiction. | BISAC FICTION / Family Life / Marriage & Divorce | FICTION / Friendship | FICTION / Romance / Contemporary Classification: LCC PS3607.A87 S53 2024 | DDC 813.6--dc23

Table of Contents

An Examined Life 6
1 Another Time and Place 7
2 Columbia Ranch 8
3 Will-Maker 12
4 The Pier 15
5 The Party 17
6 Cate's 21
7 Martini Shot 24
8 Professional Film Acting 28
9 Coming Attractions 32
10 Philosopher "Pi" 46
11 City of Diablo 50
12 San Diego 57
13 Beer and Corn Nuts 62
14 Italian Brother 66
15 Rhythm of the Night 72
16 Movie Star 79
17 Transition 86
18 Little Girl Lost 92
19 Solitude 101
20 My Sister's Keeper 114
21 Friends and Lovers 117

Table of Contents

22 Kyle's Best Friend 122
23 Edward's Wedding 128
24 The Shoot 132
25 1992 142
26 Happy 21st 143
27 Perfect Fit 149
28 A Southern Gentleman 153
29 Chicken Soup 161
30 The Other Man 165
31 What Haunts in the Night 176
32 Hold the Line 182
33 Vista 190
34 The Casita 197
35 The Call 210
36 Listen to Your Heart 212
37 Soul's Journey 219
38 Time After Time 223
Preview: *Hero Shot* 227
Exclusive Bonus: *Wonderwall - The Movie* 228
About the Author... 241

Dedicated to the child in all of us who holds fast to dreams and possibilities, despite what the world may offer.

Slating: The clapperboard used at the start of filming each scene, also called a marker or slate board. It designates vital information such as date, roll, scene, and take and ensures that audio is synced by the sound of the clapper stick snapping closed.

Magic Hour: The brief window of time just before sunrise or after sunset when the sun is not visible. Yet, its light is diffused evenly, creating a magical effect that makes it easy to light subjects evenly and quite beautifully.

An Examined Life ...

Choice, Not Chance, Determines Your Destiny.
-Aristotle

The fourth novel in the *Back to One* series—*Slating Magic Hour*—is an adventure that begs the question, *What If?*

In my debut novel—*Back to One*—the fortuitous meeting of the handsome, charming movie star, Kyle Weston, and the beautiful outsider, Catherine Leigh, alters their lives forever. Their connection is immediate and undeniable. They dare to develop a profound friendship based on respect, understanding, and sexual boundaries. A platonic relationship that is rare and nearly mythical.

I believe it is a common experience to wonder what could have been if we were to meet that special someone at a younger age. When we love someone so deeply, we selfishly wish we had more time with them earlier.

Back to One: Take 4 Slating Magic Hour takes us back sixteen years to introduce the two friends sooner in their lives and careers. Kyle, only twenty-four, is an up-and-coming star, and Cate, just eighteen, has moved to Hollywood to start an acting career. Will their youth derail their potential friendship or stifle their budding love? Or perhaps it would give them what they dreamed—more years together.

-Antonia

Chapter 1
Another Time and Place

Together, Cate and Kyle laid back, side by side, on the small dune in front of the beach house, watching the ocean sunset. Appreciating their idyllic life together, Kyle posed the wonder within the winds of time. "I wish I had known you when you first came to Hollywood. I would've been there for you if you'd let me."

She pushed up on her arms. "Of course I would. I trusted you from the moment I met you." She giggled. "What makes you think you'd even pay attention to me at that age?"

"What do you mean?"

"C'mon Kyle. I was awkward and shy and not your typical Hollywood actress. I don't think you'd even notice me. And what were you doing at twenty-four, *Mister Backseat-of-the-car*?"

"Becoming a celebrity and dating lots of women. But seriously, I would've fallen madly in love with you just as I did the night I met you at the Beverly Hills party. We were destined to be together. Either early or later, it didn't matter." He drew her close. "I'd like to imagine if I'd known you then, I'd have wrapped my arms around you and protected you forever."

Cate smiled at the fantasy. "It would've been wonderful."

She laid her head on his shoulder as he held her tenderly, observing the sun dip below the horizon, leaving the perfect blend of light and color drenching the sky.

Chapter 2
Columbia Ranch

The *Columbia Ranch* sign dwarfed the front guard gate. After checking her name on the list, security waved in the brand-new 1989 Honda Civic. As instructed, Cate parked adjacent to an unused soundstage, her radio playing Eddie Money's *I Wanna Go Back*. Tapping the steering wheel in time to the beat of the music, the eighteen-year-old took a moment to view the magical world she had just entered. She took a deep breath, holding back the exhilaration of her childhood dream coming true!

It was overwhelming when Cate's agent secured a coveted spot for her at Edna Wayne's Acting Studio. Yet here she was, entering the large stage door with her portfolio in one hand and resume in the other. It felt surreal.

The class was already in full swing when she entered. Edna Wayne, an attractive woman in her mid-sixties, turned and gestured to an empty seat in the front row.

"It's vital to be the role," she lectured to an attentive assembly of young actors. "You *are* the name on the page. You breathe life into it. Believe you're every bit of the reality of the character."

Edna moved to her front desk and skimmed the roll sheet, putting a checkmark next to a name. She looked steadfastly at the new arrival. "So tonight, class, we have Ms. Catherine Leigh believing she might join our merry little band. It's not that easy, my dear. You must prove yourself." Holding a worn, frayed-edged script for all to view, she directed, "I want you to perform this audition script ... my favorite."

Cate's eyes widened as the class began to snicker. She scanned their amused faces. A lanky fellow in his mid-twenties with dark hair, brown eyes, and a sunshine-size grin sitting next to her was more accepting.

"It'll be okay," he said in a low voice. "Have fun."

"Mr. Beason," interrupted Edna, "since you have so much to say, you may take the friend's part and read with Ms. Leigh."

"Sure." He coughed. "I'd love to."

Again, there was a wave of hushed titters as Edna signaled for the two actors to come up front, handing them the scripts.

Staring at the sides, Cate asked, "May I have a minute to look it over, please?"

"Excellent, Ms. Leigh!" Edna praised. "Did you hear that, class? Make sure you follow her example when you go out on an audition. You should never read cold-cold. Always ask for a minute to review the audition material." Turning to Cate, she added, "But no, you can't. Here you'll come up and perform ice cold."

Unsure, Cate flashed concern. "May I ask what it's about? Who *am* I?"

"What did you hear me lecture when you first came in? Show me *you* on the page. Bring it to life." The coach dramatically swept her arm, heading to sit in an empty front-row chair. "You may open the script when you're ready."

Peeking up while drawing a soothing breath, she turned the page. It was blank.

Instinctively, Cate faced her partner; her eyes sparkled mischievously.

"So tell me, will this class really help my career?"

With a huge smile, he replied, "Definitely, many students have become very successful actors."

"Ohhh," Cate said boldly, "Well then, I guess I'll stay."

Applauding loudly, Edna seized the script from Cate. She opened it to the last page. Written in big letters were the words, *You've Been Cast!*

Everybody cheered with a mixture of whistles and laughter.

"All right, class," Edna took control of the disruption, "let's have a ten-minute break."

The students began to mingle among themselves.

Turning to Cate, she generously acclaimed, "Congratulations, my dear. Not many people can handle my little test. I've seen your reel. You'll do well in this class."

The lanky fellow gave Edna back his copy of the script and again took a seat beside Cate.

"Well done," he said. "Most people get thrown by the blank page and break character. She hates that. You gotta be able to improvise."

"Thanks for your help," she said shyly.

"Catherine, I'm Joseph Beason." He extended his hand to shake.

She gleefully accepted, her expression brightening. "Nice to meet you."

Filling Cate in about the class and what to expect, Joseph was distracted by the matter flooding his mind: *How old is she? Such a baby face ... maybe fifteen? No, she must be older than that ... she reminds me of my cousin in high school. Precious and unworldly.*

He immediately felt protective.

The class resumed, and Cate was able to do some readings from actual film scripts. For her first session, she felt comfortable, primarily due to Joseph's kindness and support. Edna recognized their blossoming friendship and assigned the two a scene for the next class. They exchanged numbers and agreed to get together later in the week to rehearse.

Chapter 3
Will-Maker

"Let's get this on tape. Please state your last name and the agency representing you, and then we'll go into the scene."

Cate had been to several of these auditions and been cast in some small projects and regional commercials, but this was her first callback for a major motion picture.

The camera rolled, and she performed her sides. The character was one she felt akin … a sister, protective of her older brother, striving to keep him from doing something he'd regret. With her brother Edward, she could more than relate.

They only had her perform the scene once, yet she felt she had laid her heart on the line, and the character was her. She felt confident about the audition.

The producer, Renny Plye, nodded to the casting director. "Ms. Leigh, nicely done."

"Thank you for the opportunity." She graciously handed the sides to the casting director as the producer's assistant, Sally, entered.

"Renny, Kyle Weston's here. Shall I show him in now?"

"No, have him go to wardrobe first. They need to take his measurements."

As an aside to Cate, he said, "Thank you again. We'll contact your agent."

Jubilant, she sprinted out to the reception area and caught sight of the back of a young man heading to another section of the building.

※

Kyle was invited to view the edited footage of the "sister" auditions. The choices were reduced to three actresses. The first two were interesting, if not predictable. It almost felt to him as if they had no siblings, no connection to the brother's character being read by the casting director. However, the third actress captivated Kyle—her sincerity and realism, her lovely auburn hair framing beautiful angelic features. His sight was glued to the screen.

"So those are our options," said Renny, setting down the remote. The screenwriter, Tad Moyre, was also in the office.

"The last one, she's incredible," Kyle grinned.

"Yes, she's good," Renny remarked dismissively. "However, we're considering the first actress."

"Why? Number three's perfect," Kyle said with an enthralled air. "What's her name again?"

"Let me see. Leigh …" The producer prevued the list. "Catherine Leigh. She's a little young and unsophisticated. It's essential for the actress who plays your sister to be more streetwise."

"Ren, I could read with them. I'm happy to do that," suggested Kyle, compelled to meet her.

"Not a bad plan, Ren," Tad agreed, glimpsing up from his notes. "It's an important character. And I prefer the third actress, as well."

"All right, I'll bring them both in," Renny agreed. "Kyle, can you be here tomorrow at two o'clock?"

"Sure." Walking to the door, he turned back before leaving.

"Thanks for letting me view them."

Renny called for his assistant, "Sally?"

"Bye, Kyle." Her voice could be heard outside Renny's office. She poked her head in the doorway. "Yes, Renny."

"Call Ms. Reynold's agent and schedule her to be here at two for a callback. And contact Catherine Leigh's agent and bring her in at noon."

"Yes, sir." She left them alone in the office.

Tad was puzzled, rattling his head to think clearly. "Why are you having Leigh come in at noon when Kyle won't be here until two?"

"Because Weston's just an actor." Grabbing the script from the conference table, he advanced to his desk.

"An actor who's box office gold," alerted Tad. "He's gonna be a huge star."

"Well, it's my final decision, not an actor's. And Reynolds has the part, not Leigh."

"But Leigh's better," Tad blustered.

"I'm sure she'll have a successful career someday. Not in this production, though. It's Reynolds." He slammed the script down on his desk, refusing to debate it further.

Opening the door, Tad hesitated. "How'll you explain to Kyle why Leigh's not reading with him?"

"Easy. She had another audition to get to, and we couldn't contact him to ask if he'd be here earlier."

Tad, irritated, left the office in a huff.

Staring at the doorway to ensure he was alone, Renny picked up the phone, speaking reservedly, "Hey, babe … Yes, I realize you have to read with Weston … It's a formality. Don't worry. I swear you have the part … We'll celebrate tonight."

Chapter 4
The Pier

The placid waves gently lapped against the pilings and broke beneath the Santa Monica Pier.

Cate and Joseph meandered down, eating lots of junk food while sightseers' children scampered by them from rides to food vendors.

"I honestly believed I had the role," said Cate dejectedly. "It was the real deal. Big screen. My first."

"But you did well at the callback?"

"I thought I did." She looked at him pitifully. "I'm so disappointed. What if I'm kidding myself, and I don't have any talent?" She took an angry bite of her soft pretzel.

"That's not true. You're good. I can tell," Joseph declared.

"Thank you." Cheerily, she changed the focus to him. "Anyway, how are you doing?"

"Big news. I was cast in a supporting role in a thriller. It's shooting next spring in New Mexico."

"Oh, Joseph, how terrific! I'm so happy for you." She impulsively hugged him, causing him to nearly drop his soda. Her warmth and unfeigned ways were refreshing to him.

"Next spring? They're casting early," she added.

"It's an indie film. They do things a little differently. They don't even have a title yet," he chuckled.

"It still amazes me how everything's put together."

"Me too. How's college?"

"It's tough doing those classes while going out on casting calls, especially since I accelerated to graduate sooner." Taking a ragged breath, she showed her exhaustion just thinking about it. "Lots of work."

"Why don't you quit?" he mumbled, a mouth stuffed with the last of his pretzel.

"Can't." Seated on a bench, she examined the ocean. "It was my mother's condition for me to move here."

"Well, can you break away for a party this Saturday night? A friend of mine's throwing a little get-together. You can use a night off."

She scrunched a doubtful face at his proposal.

"I'm recommending it as a pal," he clowned. "We're pals, aren't we?"

"Yes, we are."

"Great. I'll give you the details so you can meet me there."

"I don't know," Cate said apprehensively, her head lowered, avoiding eye contact. "Industry people intimidate me. They always seem to be after something."

"Yeah, that's because they are. Seriously, this business has a horrible way of causing extreme self-doubt. Your problem is you're way too nice for this town." He then noticed her concern. "I pledge I'll be a faithful friend and won't abandon you."

"Joseph, you're my only one here in town," she smiled, touching his arm lightly.

Strolling toward the parking lot, he grabbed his small finger in hers. "Pinky swear. Friends for life, agreed?"

"Yeah." She had a joyous look.

Chapter 5
The Party

Loud music and chatter seeped through the open front door. A sea of people—most unfamiliar faces—received Joseph as he weaved through the crowd to find Kyle in his kitchen, handing out beer to a line of guests.

"You need a bigger place if you're gonna have this many people."

"Hey, Joseph," greeted Kyle. "I think Jacqueline invited them. I didn't. They keep showing up."

"You're still with her?" Joseph reclined against the closed refrigerator.

"Not a fan, huh?" Kyle laughed, handing two bottles to the last couple in line.

"Not at all." He crossed his arms stubbornly. "She's awfully demanding for my taste."

"I guess it's good she's my girl, not yours." Kyle repositioned the beer and sodas in the two large coolers. "Speaking of that, are you dating anyone since what's-her-name?"

"Nope, but I made a friend. A nice girl in my acting class."

"Not girlfriend material?" He plucked out a beer and gave it to Joseph.

"Oh, hell no. Too young and sweet. She needs someone to watch out for her, like a big brother. That's what I am—a big brother."

"How old is this girl?"

"She's eighteen." Joseph wiggled his hand at the statement. "Except she's not Hollywood eighteen if ya know what I mean. She's exceptionally naïve."

"So, Joseph," he asked craftily, "you won't be nailing her?"

"No, I'm making sure no one else tries to."

"Kyle!" Jacqueline yelled while motioning to a doorway. She was tall and striking, a twenty-something woman with medium-length black hair and a haughty strut.

Joseph looked the other way.

"Duty calls." Opening a beer, Kyle took a swig and handed it to his friend. Holding the two bottles, Joseph watched Jacqueline drag Kyle into the bedroom, closing the door behind them.

Searching the packed room, Joseph spotted Cate entering, smiling self-consciously, appearing very much out of place.

He made his way to the center of the room. "You're here."

"Yeah, I can't stay long, though," she said tentatively, overwhelmed by the crowd of strangers. "I have a paper due Monday."

He inclined closer to her to hear over the music and loud voices. "I'm pleased you came. Wanna drink?"

Staring at the two bottles in his hands, she guessed he was offering her one. "I … um … don't like the taste of beer."

Joseph detected he was still holding Kyle's. "No, this is my buddy's," he responded, setting it down on the nearby table.

"Are there any sodas?" she asked, glancing toward the kitchen.

"Sure, c'mon, I know my way around." Leading her into the kitchen, they dug into the coolers of drinks.

Cate looked about the room. "Whose place is this anyway?"

"A friend's. I'd introduce you, but he's a little preoccupied at the moment." He handed her a bottle of Sprite.

Gavrihel

"It's a cute residence for Studio City." Nodding toward the mob, she twisted the screw top to open the soda. "Who're all these people? Industry?"

"Yeah, some. Most are here for a good time."

Strangers kept hailing Joseph. He acknowledged their greetings as they strolled out of the kitchen.

"You're popular," she noted, jiggling the bottle nervously.

"I go out on a lot of auditions."

She spoke close to his ear, refraining from shouting, "How long'll you be in New Mexico filming?"

"About three weeks, but not until the end of April."

"Darn, you'll miss my birthday."

"We'll celebrate when I get back." Hesitantly, he probed, "Nineteen, right?"

"Yeah."

Her smile melted his heart, beguiling him.

"Excuse me for a second," he uttered, "Nature calls."

Quickly stepping away from the impulse, he shook his head. "God, she's *so* beautiful," he fussed to himself.

⥊

Alone in the horde of partiers, Cate had two different guys come up and flirt with her. Shyness paralyzing her, she excused herself on both occasions, taking refuge at the far side of the room. Pressed against the wall—a true wallflower—she was surprised as a terrier puppy sniffed her foot, happily wagging his tail.

"Well, hi there. Who're you?" She sat down in the corner on the floor, and the dog jumped on her lap. Reading the tag hanging from his collar, she greeted, "Hey, Pepper. You're sure cute." He licked her chin and made himself cozy in her lap. Absentmindedly, Cate stroked his fur, Pepper enjoying the care.

Coming out of the bathroom, Joseph was cornered by some

associates. He made every effort to see above and beyond the crowd to locate Cate.

Still seated on the floor with Pepper snuggling on her lap, Cate, too, was watching for Joseph's return. She looked around the room. Guests in clusters packing every inch, music blaring in the background, *Hungry Like the Wolf* by Duran Duran. She spied a couple making out on the sofa a few feet from where she sat. Tension prickled her senses. She saw Joseph delayed by acquaintances, unable to extricate himself. Uneasy, she again noticed the love birds on the sofa, entangled in each other's arms, and instead forced her concentration on Pepper, who was licking her hand.

Abruptly, Pepper's head popped up, staring at something on the other side of the room. Hopping off Cate's lap, he sprinted through the attendees' legs, jumping up and down to get Kyle's attention.

Kyle picked him up. "Hey, how did you get out of the bedroom?" Glancing in the direction Pepper had traveled, the crowd having temporarily parted like the red sea, he saw Cate stand up, cleaning off the puppy's fur from her lap.

"Look who *you* found," he said to the dog with an amplified grin.

Cate set down her soda and hurried to the door.

"Wait!" he called. The music and voices were at a roar, making it impossible to be heard. By the time he dodged his way past the partiers to the door, Pepper in his arms, she was gone.

Chapter 6
Cate's

Edward plopped onto the sofa, amused as his sister ecstatically twirled around the room.

"Thank you, Ed. The concert was awesome. Eric Clapton's such an amazing artist, and what a nice man."

"Yeah, he is. It was refreshing not having to hide you behind me. Oh, here's your concert tee-shirt." He tossed her an oversized shirt. "It's all they had left."

Cate held out the XL tee-shirt. "I can sleep in it. Thanks. How's work?"

"Good."

She sat next to him, cross-legged. "And law school?"

"Kicking my butt," he grumbled, flopping his legs onto the ottoman. "I hope I can pass the Bar. The exam scares me."

Folding the tee-shirt, she set it on the lamp table. "Ed, you're in your third year. You have to graduate first."

"It's all good." He rubbed his forehead, appearing miserable. "Well, not totally. Valerie's getting pushy to get married."

Cate tossed her head back in frustration. "Ed, please," she griped, "can't you get a better girlfriend?"

"Why? She's pretty and smart," he replied almost mechanically.

Cate sprung up to grab the water pitcher from the refrigerator, pouring a glass for herself. "She's smart all right. She's using you." Indicating her drink, she asked, "Want some water?"

He shook his head no. "Using me?" He wormed into the

softness of the sofa, trying to find a more comfortable position.
"For what?"
Strolling back to him, she set her drink on the side table. "Your future. You have a great future ahead of you."
"No, you're wrong." Edward snitched a sip from her glass. "She's not like that."
"I'm not wrong, Ed. I want you to be happy. There's someone better out there for you. My goodness, what about a pretty law student? You'd have something in common, at least."
"Law students only have studying on their minds," he simpered, taking a long drink from the glass. "No extracurricular activities."
She raised her eyes to the ceiling. "Whatever. Don't take my advice then."
Swallowing another sip, he asked, "How about you?"
"Me?" Copying his posture on the sofa, she reached for his still-clutched water glass.
"Are you dating anyone?"
"No! My schedule's way too full! There's not a second between auditions and getting through college as quickly as possible. I'm taking more than a full load each semester."
"Catherine Leigh, you overachieving bookworm," he laughed. "Weren't you like sixteen when you signed up for a bunch of classes at the junior college?"
"Uh-huh. I was trying to get a jump on college."
Tipping the empty water glass, she glared at him for drinking it all.
"Sorry." He snatched it from her hand and went to the kitchen to refill the glass. "Why not enjoy it? Have fun. College's where I met girls!"
"I'm not you," she rejoined.
"I'm just concerned for your well-being, Sis. Alone in L.A. Have you made any friends?"

"Yes, in my acting class."

"That's good. Hate to think of you locking yourself up to study in this apartment every night and watching TV in place of a social life." He drank some water before handing her the glass. She fidgeted, realizing her brother knew her well. She was doing precisely that.

"This has been fun," he said, "but I need to get some sleep before work tomorrow. Thanks for going with me tonight."

"Thank you for taking me," she beamed, following him to the door.

He sniffed the air. "By the way, why is it stuffy in here?"

She flinched. "The window unit's broken."

Edward got right into her face. "Did you tell the apartment manager?"

"Yes, he said he'd get around to it. That was a week ago." She stared self-consciously at the floor.

"That's not acceptable! Do you need me to call him?"

She gripped her brother's arm. "Would you? He listens to you."

"Only because I make him do his job. This is why I told Mom you're too young to be on your own. Catherine, you pay rent. You're entitled to an air-conditioned apartment. Be more assertive," he scolded as she winced pathetically.

Edward, realizing his anger was misplaced, became more understanding. It wasn't his sister's fault people took advantage of her sweetness and youth.

"I'll handle it." He opened the door. "Hey, Bon Jovi announced they're doing a concert here next June with WeSheim opening for them. Do you want me to see if I can snag some tickets for us?"

"Yes, thank you! Love you."

Chapter 7
Martini Shot

The spring air poured through the doorway of the somewhat drab establishment. Sitting at the corner table, Kyle and Joseph swigged their cold beer.

"Finally, it's in the can," Joseph laughed. "Man, you've been working on this one for a long time."

"Technical difficulties and a cast member who required lots of directing," Kyle complained as he sat back casually.

"So, when's the premiere?"

"Memorial Day weekend," he said, taking a pretzel from the dish in the center of the table.

Feeling obligated to ask about his least favorite person, Joseph prodded, "Is Jacqueline excited to go with you?"

"Nah, we broke up. It was getting weird."

"About time!" said Joseph, unusually upbeat. "She was such a ballbuster."

Kyle brought the bottle to his lips. "She left me for someone with more pull in the business."

Dumbfounded, Joseph stared at him. "Ouch!"

"She was trying to get me to use my influence to get her a part in my next film. I've already found her an agent and introduced her to several powerful people. I spend enough time with her already. I don't want to see her every day on set. When I said I wouldn't, she found somebody who would."

"Using you. Okay, I get it."

"Anyway, it's over," he firmly asserted.

The waitress strolled by. Pointing at their nearly empty beer bottles, Joseph motioned for another round.

"So, you're on the prowl again?" needled Joseph.

"Prowl?" Kyle frowned, looking at him sideways. "Not my style. But I do need a date for the premiere. An old friend from Costa Mesa moved to town. I might bring her."

"Have I met this one?" Joseph crouched forward, elbows on the table.

"No, we dated in high school. Julia Morris. I've been debating whether we should get together again. She's hot, smart, nice. But …" He scrunched his nose. "She's after a ring."

"Wow, a commitment to something other than your career?" Joseph smirked, "That's not happening."

Restlessly, Kyle broke the pretzel into several small pieces and brushed the salt from his hands. "I don't fall in love. It's a waste of time. And it never seems to end well."

"Kyle, you're the king of flings. Now, me, I have real relationships."

"Yeah, and you're the one always getting dumped."

"Hey!" Sitting back quickly, Joseph's eyes were large. "That's low, Kyle. True but low."

"Well, in sheer numbers, buddy, you've had a lot more women than me."

Joseph pulled back his shoulders and smugly grinned. "And I'm not even a superstar with girls throwing themselves at me."

"At least I'm never alone. Sex does fill the emptiness."

Shaking his head, Joseph coolly assessed. "Interesting. Have you ever mentioned your stand on love and relationships before you bang them?"

Kyle shrugged, peeling the label from his beer bottle.

"No wonder you're the cover boy for every tabloid in town," Joseph continued. "Afraid of love?"

"Not afraid. I'm not interested in the hassle."

Joseph reclined with his arm slung along the back of the chair. "You might wanna reconsider taking your old high school hookup to the premiere who's marriage-bound when all you want is to get laid."

"Who says that's all I want?" he posed with a devilish grin.

Jiggling his beer bottle, Joseph squinted. "I do, Kyle, 'cause I know you. You're only kidding yourself."

He grunted at him with a laugh. "Enough about me ... how's your love life?"

"You mean right now at this very moment?" Hiding his mouth behind the bottle, Joseph stalled. "Nonexistent."

Eying him suspiciously, Kyle was entertained by his pal's predicament. "What about your little friend?"

"She's still a friend. I know that sounds crazy to you." He vacillated. "Seriously though, she's a wonderful actress. She outperforms the other students, and no one comes close to her. Too good for this town." Looking around the half-empty bar, he moved in closer. "I worry for her. When she goes out on auditions, it makes me nervous. She tells me what some of the industry guys say to her. She has no clue they're hitting on her."

"You do sound like an older brother. What's wrong with you? What makes this girl so special?"

"The point I'm making is that she's incredibly gullible."

"Joseph, some people don't belong in L.A., no matter how gifted. Maybe she should stick to community theater."

"Now, who's a misanthrope?"

Kyle stared at him, stumped.

Whimsically, Joseph tipped the bottle to his lips. "It means cynic. Expand your vocabulary, Kyle. Read a book."

"You're an ass," he chuckled.

"I'm saying you should stop dating starlets who only care if you're helping them with their careers. It's making you bitter."

Kyle slid forward, pointing his finger for emphasis. "Yeah,

you're probably right. Maybe a girl like Julia's someone I should be dating."

Matching his urgency, Joseph moved forward as well. "Isn't there anyone else you've met since you became a household name?"

"No." He hesitated, then sighed. "Except there's this one actress. I saw the tape of her audition a few months ago. She was amazing, and then she came to the party I threw last fall. She left before I could meet her. There was something about her."

"Too bad she left. Did you get her name?"

"Yeah, I did," he said with a tone of realization.

"So, ask your agent if he can track her down for you."

"Good idea, Joseph," he grinned. "That college education has come in handy."

"UCLA ... more semesters than you, superstar."

"Fame called."

Putting his thumb and index finger so they nearly touched, Joseph held up his hand. "You've come this close to meeting that girl twice. It's destiny. That reminds me, Edna wanted me to ask you to speak to the class next week. You showing up gives her credibility as one of her success stories."

Kyle snickered pompously. "So, Joseph, are you ever gonna graduate from acting classes?"

"I'm keeping sharp until my big break. Anyway, I've seen your work. You might wanna take a refresher course," bantered Joseph with a laugh.

"Tell Edna, sure, I'm free. And I can meet your little sister," he jibed.

"Ha-ha, funny."

Chapter 8
Professional Film Acting

Edna received her former student as if he were the prodigal son returning. The class took their seats. Kyle's back to the class, he and Edna were engrossed in a discourse over Columbia Ranch being absorbed by Warner Brothers, soon-to-be renamed Warner Ranch.

The door opened, and Cate ran to take her seat beside Joseph. Looking beyond Kyle while handing him a newspaper column highlighting the class, Edna scolded, "My dear, you're late."

"I'm terribly sorry," said Cate, out of breath. "Traffic was horrible, Ms. Wayne."

"No excuses."

"Yes, ma'am."

"It's unbelievable to hear manners these days," said Edna delightedly in a low voice to Kyle, occupied by the article.

Stepping forward, Edna addressed the seated students. "Well, class, now that Ms. Leigh has graced us with her presence, we can begin."

When Kyle heard *Ms. Leigh*, he whirled around, scanning the class to find Cate sitting with Joseph.

"Class, we have one of my former students visiting today. Someone, I'm sure, with whom his work you're familiar, Kyle Weston."

Kyle stood before the group. His sight remained on Cate.

"It's nice to be here. I owe much of my success to this

extraordinary acting instructor, Edna Wayne." Wrestling to pull his attention from Cate, Kyle was unexpectedly at a loss for words.

Joseph crossly grimaced as he recognized the "object" of Kyle's intense focus.

Regaining his senses, Kyle discussed the career path challenges and how to navigate the business. Students began to raise posturing queries. He handled them calmly, fighting the urge to stare at the beautiful girl with auburn hair and brown eyes.

※

When the session ended and the class began to disperse, female students surrounded Kyle. The women avidly attempted to trap his interest under the pretense of asking him to clarify points he had made in his lecture. He kept sneaking a peek at Cate. When he saw her collecting her things to leave, he pithily excused himself and rushed to his buddy.

"Hey, Joseph," he said hastily.

"Yeah." Joseph stepped forward, hindering Kyle's access to his friend.

"Aren't you going to …" Intimating toward Cate, Kyle winked his eye.

Joseph took an exasperated breath. "Catherine Leigh, this is Kyle Weston."

She smiled brightly. "Hello."

"You were at my party," Kyle said, becoming entranced.

"I was?" She glanced at Joseph, who took an edgy breath, glaring at Kyle.

Finally, he confirmed, "Yeah, that was Kyle's party."

"Oh," she said sprightly, "you have a cute place and lots of friends. I love your puppy."

"The house is a rental," said Kyle, his gaze locked on Cate. "I didn't know most of the people there."

Edna called from her desk, "Ms. Leigh, may I see you up front, please?"

"Pardon me. Good meeting you." As she padded up to Edna's desk, Kyle followed her with his eyes.

"That's *her*," he muttered, frozen in awe.

"I gathered that," groaned Joseph. "Kyle, stay away from her, please."

"C'mon, Joseph. She's ..."

"Perfect. So let it go," demanded Joseph.

Cate returned with a script, alive with anticipation. "Joseph, Ms. Wayne assigned this scene. How 'bout working on it with me?"

For Kyle, nearly hypnotized by her essence, the attraction seemed to compound each moment he watched her.

"Sure," Joseph said sharply, scrutinizing Kyle's expression. "Why don't we leave now and run the scene."

"I can't tonight," she chuckled at her acting partner's nonsensical suggestion—it was already so late. "I need to go home and study for a test tomorrow."

"Fine, so we'll talk later." Joseph jammed her purse into her arms and nudged her toward the door.

"Ms. Leigh, it was very nice to meet you," said Kyle rather zealously.

As she was leaving, her brow knitted with a curious flash. Replaying the last few moments in her mind, she shook her clouded head, passing it off as the odd behavior of actors.

Kyle wheeled around to Joseph. "What the hell?! Why were you trying to get her away from me? She's not your girlfriend!"

"She's my friend." Joseph began to pick up his script and notes, placing them in his backpack.

Without forethought, Kyle spewed, "So why cock-block me?"

"That's exactly why you shouldn't be around her," he explicitly stated. "She's not for you. Period! You get plenty of tail out there."

Kyle awkwardly backpedaled. "Hey, maybe I wasn't thinking of her in that way. Did you ever consider that?"

"Seriously?! We both know what's on your mind. She's gorgeous."

"Yes, but there's more there than that. I saw her tape. She's wonderful. I appreciate her talent."

"Sure, her talent," Joseph mocked. "That's what caused you not to be able to string two coherent sentences together talking to her."

"You're exaggerating," he said heatedly.

"Yes, I am … to make a point. She's too good for you." Zipping up his backpack, Joseph slung it over his shoulder.

Annoyed, Kyle snipped, "You're not giving me her phone number?"

"No way in hell." Defiantly, he looked away.

"Fine." Kyle walked up to Edna and whispered in her ear. She laughed, opened her roll book, and handed him a sheet of paper.

"Damn it!" grumbled Joseph.

Chapter 9
Coming Attractions

As Cate began to leave for her morning class, she was startled by the phone. Turning back, unsettled, she answered, "Hello."

"Good morning, Ms. Leigh," a friendly male voice began. "This is Kyle."

"Who?"

"Kyle. Kyle Weston."

"Oh, hello." Her mind questioned, *Kyle Weston ... why is he calling me?* "I enjoyed your lecture last night."

"It was wonderful to meet you."

"Is there something I can help you with?" she replied cautiously, glimpsing down at her wristwatch.

"I was wondering if you'd have lunch with me?"

"That's sweet of you to ask. Unfortunately, I don't have a lunch hour. I've got classes at UCLA most of the day. Maybe some other time."

"I'd really like to see you today," he petitioned sincerely. "Could we meet in between classes? Please." His voice was remarkably genuine.

She lagged. Although his life was splashed on checkout counter magazines with sensational headlines, she didn't know him. "I guess we can meet on campus. I have a break between 3:15 and 4:00."

"Sure. Where will you be?"

"The theater," she denoted uncertainly.
"Great. I know it well. See you there."

Kyle arrived forty-five minutes early and roamed around the campus. His old stomping ground for three semesters. As the first autograph seeker clamored for his attention, he realized college life was certainly not the same as years ago. Being swarmed by the rewards of fame felt claustrophobic. Wearily, he excused himself from the small but vocal amassing of female fans to the safety of the theater.

Sitting in the top row in the darkness, he watched Cate on stage rehearsing with two other students. She was vibrant, playful, and full of life. He understood why Joseph was reluctant to share her. There was something graceful and yet fragile in her being. It made him feel a bit boyish.

When class ended, the stocky professor with salt and pepper hair in his mid-fifties called her over to speak. The other students were gone. As far as the teacher knew, they were utterly alone. Sliding forward in his seat, Kyle strained to hear what was being said. This conversation struck him as peculiar. Cate was visibly unnerved and kept backing away. He could no longer sit still, leaping up and tramping down the aisle to the front of the stage.

When she saw him, her disconcerted expression turned to joy.

"Mr. Greco, I have to go. Thanks for the advice," she said.

She ran down the aisle to greet him.

Kyle whispered, "You all right?"

"Uh-huh," she answered hurriedly.

Racing outside to the picturesque grounds, he trailed behind. The balminess of the sun caressed their faces on this pleasant spring day. Her stride was steady and fast until she was far from the theater. Kyle tried to keep up.

"Thanks for coming here," she said.

"What did he say to you?" he asked, needing to clarify what he had witnessed.

"Who?"

"Your professor."

"Nothing," she downplayed. "And he's not a professor—he's an acting coach. Let's talk about something else."

"Okay, so here we are. I'm happy you decided to join me."

She tipped her head slightly. "Why wouldn't I?"

"I mean, you found time to spend with me. I appreciate it." They ventured to the common area. "You met my dog, Pepper, at my party. He really likes you. And I looked for you, but you were gone."

"Pepper's such a cute puppy."

"He's a character. And smart." Kyle flattered impishly, "He picked you out of the crowd."

Cate blushed.

"So, tell me about yourself," he began. "Where're you from?"

"What makes you think I'm not from here?" She elicited a befuddled expression from him, which she found flirtatious. "You're right," she giggled, "I'm from San Diego. My mother still lives there, but my brother's up here. He's in law school."

"I could tell you have a brother," he said.

Stunned, she prompted, "Why would you think that?"

"From your audition for *Will-Maker*." Passing an ornamental orange tree whose blossoms had nearly turned to budded fruit, Kyle picked a petal and held it to his nose. Then offered it to Cate with an amiable swagger.

"You were terrific," he continued. "You understood the character and her motivation."

Pleasantly enticed, she inhaled the citrusy fragrance, unconsciously rubbing the petal on the inside of her wrist.

Kyle was fascinated by her actions, nodding toward her arm. "May I?"

"Oh," she said, cheeks radiantly flushing, and extended her arm. He held her hand, breathing in the sweet scent of orange blossom upon her soft skin.

"You smell good," he smiled, his deep blue eyes mesmerizing her.

Slipping her hand from his, she exhaled, rattled, returning to the subject. "So, you saw my audition?"

"They showed me the top contenders. You were my first choice."

She was astounded. "Too bad you didn't have a say in casting."

"I kind of did." He touched her arm gently to get her attention. "That's why I requested to read with you on the final callback."

Bewilderment reflected in Cate's eyes. "But you never showed."

"Yes, I did." He was puzzled. "You came early because of your other audition."

"I didn't have another audition. My callback was at noon."

He roused his sight upward, aggravated. "Renny."

She gave a questioning frown.

"The producer," he explained. "He set it up so we wouldn't meet. He planned to cast his girlfriend in the part. You were in the way."

"Oh. I guess that's the business. I won't let it get to me. Hope she did well."

"It was … ya know …" He pursed his lips. "It's still a fine film."

"When does it open?" she asked.

"Memorial Day weekend."

"Oh, that's good. A holiday weekend." With a fragile sigh, her smile bloomed, the sunlight illuminating her loveliness.

Perhaps it was how she gazed at him … his breath caught in his chest. *My God,* he thought, *she's even more beautiful than when I first saw her.* His eyes brightened. "Cate, would you like to go to the premiere with me?"

"What?" She was floored. "Are you joking?!"

"I'm serious."

"But we don't know each other."

"We could get acquainted," he suggested eagerly.

Cate stiffened, backing away a few steps.

"No," he quickly revised. "I didn't mean it that way." Reaching out, he reassured, "As friends."

His words brought an endearing smile to her lips, feeling a kinship.

"The more I work in this business and become recognized," he added, "the less I trust the people near me. Everyone wants something. No one has a conversation. Not one without an agenda, anyway. Joseph's the one true friend I have because we go back to the beginning."

"He's a good friend."

"Did he tell you we met here at UCLA? I went for a couple years before things broke for me. Joseph almost graduated until acting became his priority." He paused. "He didn't …" Halting his words, he immediately deemed it unwise to tell her that Joseph had been furious about Kyle knowing Cate.

"He didn't what?" She fished for the rest of the comment.

Rapidly, he changed the subject. "What're you doing after class tonight?"

"Studying and sleeping. I have an audition tomorrow."

"Saturday night then?"

"Oh, going to a concert with my brother."

"How about Sunday?" he persisted.

"Well …" She reasoned for a moment. "If I get my studying done tonight, nothing."

"You like baseball?"

"I love baseball." Cate was thrilled by the prospect of sitting in the cool springtime sun. "My dad was a die-hard Cubs fan."

"Dodgers are playing the Padres," he said excitedly. "Hey, you're from San Diego. You get to see Tony Gwynn. And we can have a fun, unhealthy lunch of hotdogs and beer. Sound good?"

"Yes!" she replied with gusto. "Except I don't drink beer. I prefer soda."
"I could pick you up to go to Dodger Stadium."
She pondered for an instant.
"As friends," he added.
Smiling, she tore a piece of paper from her notebook and wrote down her address, giving it to him. "Here."
"You live in Toluca Lake?"
"Don't be impressed. It's a small apartment complex next to the freeway. It's technically North Hollywood."
"First pitch is 1:00. Pick you up at 11:30?"
Cate smiled broadly. "Great."
"I'll see you then."
Two days ... an eternity, he mulled.

It turns out Kyle loved the Dodgers and Cate the Padres. It made the game more fun—they each respected the other's passion. Having a deep understanding of the game, as Cate did, impressed Kyle. The Dodgers won 4-2.

They strolled to Kyle's new 1990 Mustang convertible. As he put the top down, Cate sported a baseball cap, cramming her long auburn hair under it.

"So, where to, milady?" He casually rested his arm on the top of the steering wheel.

"Not dinner. I'm stuffed. I can't believe I ate a hotdog and ice cream and a huge soft pretzel!" she said with a chuckle.

"How about a movie?" He cut his eyes to glimpse her reaction.

"Great!" She lit up. "We can have popcorn."

"Weren't you full?" he laughed.

"You can't go to a movie without popcorn. It's basically air."

He reflected, "I've been working and behind on my movies. Have you seen *Hunt for Red October*?"

"Not yet," she said zestfully. "Let's go."

He turned on the FM radio, and a Todd Rundgren tune played.

Glee spread over her face. "Ahh, *I Saw the Light*. I love this song! I have such great memories. Laying out in the sun at the beach on a summer day and counting shooting stars later at night."

Kyle was smitten. "*Cause I saw the light in your eyes*," he sang. "Very sweet."

"Yeah, pretty innocent stuff, I know," she said shyly. "Okay, your turn. What's your best memory of this tune?"

"Well, I wasn't innocent," he smiled. "Memory ... hmm ... my first make-out session with Susie Dexter. We were twelve, listening to the radio in her backyard."

"Fascinating," she giggled.

He jumped into the song.

But my feelings for you were just something I never knew
'Til I saw the light ...

He stopped and glanced at Cate with an earnest smile. "Good song. Sing."

Cate slowly turned her head. "No way. I don't sing in front of people."

"I'm not people. I'm a friend. Come on, sing with me." He carried on singing loudly, coaxing her. Brushing aside a strand of hair that had escaped her ball cap, his tone was ludicrous. However, his goofy persuasion worked, and Cate began to meekly sing.

"You have a lovely voice," he complimented in between verses.

∞

They sat in the middle-middle with a jumbo popcorn and a large drink. The previews had yet to start, but the theater was not particularly crowded for a new release.

Cate again wondered why he was being so considerate to her. From what she had seen standing at the grocery store checkout line—headlines in the magazine everywhere touting his roguish nature—he didn't seem like that at all. It made her question what he wanted. What did *she* want? She looked into his caring eyes—so blue—shaking away her hesitancy.

"So, you enjoy movies," began Kyle.

"No, I love movies. I don't care what decade. I believe I've seen them all. I can quote lines from my favorites," she said rather cheekily.

"Such as?"

Striving to recall, she exhaled thoughtfully. "There're the famous ones like Rhett Butler saying, *Frankly, my dear, I don't give a damn.* Or Benjamin Braddock saying, *Mrs. Robinson, you're trying to seduce me. Aren't you?*" She acted relatively self-assured.

He laughed, "Interesting. *Gone with the Wind* and *The Graduate.*"

"Correct," she agreed. "How about *Life moves pretty fast. If you don't stop and look around once in a while, you could miss it.*"

Kyle thought hard to recall the quote, snapping his fingers. "Oh, I should know this."

"*Ferris Bueller*," Cate revealed with a knowing look.

"Right." He examined her fervor. "How come you remember the guys' lines?"

"Men's roles are usually more colorful." She slumped down in her seat and munched on the popcorn they shared. She motioned for his drink, which he indecisively handed to her.

"I offered to buy you a drink."

"I'd rather have some of yours," she said coquettishly, munching more popcorn as the lights faded and the action on the screen seized her attention.

He'd glanced at her often as strange emotions were developing in him. Every time he tried to shake off the sensation, they would return more robust. There was a precious vibrancy in her enthusiasm that was impossible to resist.

※

Walking Cate to her door, Kyle felt awkward—a new experience for him.

"Thanks for today," she said jovially.

"You're welcome." Once more, there was an overpowering need to see her again as soon as possible. "Wanna hang out tomorrow?"

"I can't. I have classes."

"Right, it's Monday. How 'bout after?" He brushed her cheek. "We could take in another movie."

Blushing from his touch, she granted, "Okay. I'll be back from class by 5:30."

"I'll pick you up at six, then."

"Thanks again," she purred, opening the door.

Slowly, Kyle leaned in to kiss her, causing Cate to bashfully duck the contact by stepping inside.

"Good night," she said and shut the door behind her.

Staring at the closed door, he snorted, "Damn."

As he climbed into his car, Kyle's mind was in overdrive. *She's beautiful ... she's alluring ... so much fun ... I really like her.*

※

They spent virtually every evening with each other, partaking in nonstop classic movies and long walks with Pepper. Surprising herself at this new focus on fun, she adjusted her studious routine.

Cate also spent time teaching the puppy tricks. He was eager to learn, easily grasping commands such as sit, roll over, and shake—with his left paw.

"You've turned my dog into a southpaw."

"He'd make a great first baseman," she replied sassily.

"Except he'd never give the ball back."

Pepper had no idea what they were talking about but happily cuddled beside them, absorbing their warmth toward each other.

Walking back into her living room, a soda in hand, Kyle saw Cate sitting on the floor with Pepper relaxing in her lap.

"Kyle, watch," she alerted. "Pepper, go to Kyle."

The dog ran to Kyle, sat by his feet, and looked to Cate for direction.

"Use your words," she encouraged the pup. Pepper raised his head and let out a muffled bark.

"See, now he'll let you know what he needs without jumping all over you."

"That's great." He joined her on the floor, their backs against the sofa, petting the dog. "And you did all this in a few days? You're amazing."

"No, Pepper's the smart one. Such a good boy." She baby-talked, hugging the pup and kissing the top of his head. Kyle studied her verve for the unplanned moments, wishing he was the recipient of her affection.

Remaining on the floor, they settled into yet another wonderful conversation. It surprised Kyle. Cate was the first girl he could talk with and unmask his true self. He poured out his heart regarding his experience as an actor and rising star in a town that could be brutal—sharing his profound emotions concerning his insecurities. And despite her youth, she was strikingly insightful and wise. It was similar to sharing aims with an old soul that happened to be connected to his. It was evident why Joseph enjoyed her friendship. She was unbelievably astute when it came to her craft and life.

On Friday afternoon, he drove them to Malibu. Kyle knew of a private access entrance to the beach. He slipped beyond the gate, helping her in. They strolled along the shallows, gazing at the shore's exquisite beach houses. Without warning, Cate stopped, looking at the most beautiful among the others.

Wistfully, she said, "Must be nice."

"You like it?"

Starry-eyed, she gasped, "Yeah, it's incredible!"

"That would be a great place to live," he mused, tossing a seashell along the beach.

He dropped onto a small sand dune in front of the beach house. She sat beside him and laid back. Basking in the sun, she was unwittingly inviting. *Joseph was right—so unassuming.* He fought the urge to kiss her.

He had to get his mind on something else. "So, you have any auditions next week?"

Pushing up on her arms, she faced him. "No, I'm filming an industrial; how to use a new telecommunication system. I must look like someone who doesn't know how to dial a phone," she joked.

"Good money?" He found an intact seashell beside his leg and placed it in Cate's hand.

"Yes! The casting director lives in my building. She's been tremendously generous." She rubbed the smoothness of the shell with her finger. "Assures me I'll be able to do it several times throughout the year. It's enough to pay my rent for quite a while!"

"That's great," he said warmly, his eyes capturing her gaze. Surrendering to the impulse, Kyle leaned in to kiss her. Again, Cate immediately pulled away, slightly turning from him, and peered down, embarrassed. He was caught off guard by her distancing.

Timidly, she spoke, "Kyle, may I please say something? I think you're the most amazing guy. So handsome, nice, and kind ... and I can't look into your blue eyes without melting."

His face glowed with curiosity at her candor. As much as he craved embracing and kissing her, he wanted to hear what she had to say ... or did he?

"You're very experienced ... so many women. You're a bit wild, and ... honestly, it's intimidating and not something I'm ready for. I have to concentrate on my studies and my work, my career. They're very important to me. It's why I moved to L.A. I must focus on ..." With a bated sigh, she swore, "I don't wanna be ... you know ..."

"Cate," he quickly started, "I don't think of you that way. The tabloids make me out to be ..."

"A rascal?" she inserted awkwardly.

"Well, I am," he admitted with a chuckle.

Subdued, she concentrated silently on the seashell.

"I'm a celebrity," he explained. "In demand ... by lots of people ... for many reasons."

She glanced up at him, her eyes so hypnotic. "And I'm just a college girl trying to break into this business the right way ... with talent."

Kyle hoped his openness would perhaps get her to reconsider. "Cate." He tipped his head to hold her sight. "You already mean more to me than anyone I've ever known." Taking her hand in his, he earnestly added, "I'm really a good guy. I never felt ... Please give me a chance. I enjoy being with you." It seemed as if his heart would explode from the ecstasy of her presence and the fear of her running away.

"I love spending time with you, too. I consider you a good friend. All my friends back home are boys ... *just* friends, nothing more. Like Joseph and me."

"You must know a lot of frustrated guys," he teased, then noticing her somber state, readjusted his manner. "Sorry."

Cate was confident her boundaries were well-founded. "It'd be so easy to be with you the other way. But I'm not ready. I'm not looking for a relationship. Not yet. I think I need time. I hope you still wanna be friends."

Taking a solemn breath, he vowed, "I don't wanna lose you. I'll wait for the most beautiful girl in the world." His eyes seemed to reflect sincerity. "Friends first."

"And always?"

Stroking her head, he again leaned in. This time giving her a quick peck on the cheek. "Yeah."

They whiled away the afternoon—sharing dreams and grand ambitions, laughing so hard it exhausted them until they beheld the sunset on the ocean waves—a magical hour.

The drive to Cate's apartment was quiet. Her eyes were closed. However, Kyle suspected she was thinking, not drifting to sleep.

He softly tapped her arm. "Cate?"

She gazed at him with an open expression.

"Tomorrow, I'll be taping interviews for *Will-Maker* and then out of town next week. I'll miss you."

"Me too. It's too bad, though. Joseph and I are meeting at the soda shop in the Valley before he leaves for New Mexico. I was gonna invite you to join us."

"Thanks, but can't," he said with a laugh. "Joseph talks about that place a lot. Let me know if the desserts are as good as he claims." He tapped the steering wheel with his thumbs, glancing at her. Adeptly, he added, "He doesn't know we've been hanging out, does he?"

"No, this'll be the first time I've even seen him since you

stopped by my theater class. Why?"

"No reason," he said prudently. "Let me tell him, okay?"

"Sure." She stared at him, baffled.

Returning to the previous subject to distract her, he said, "Anyway, I'm meeting with producers in New York. I'll call you when I return."

"Have a good trip."

※

After seeing Cate safely to her apartment, Kyle began driving to his home, ambushed by a rush of thoughts. *Joseph was wrong. I'm not totally self-absorbed. I can be a close friend with a female beyond sex.*

Kyle had to admire Cate's drive and focus to succeed. He could relate to her passion for her craft. It was the same for him since he began his career. Women were only an enjoyable distraction. Never a commitment, as it would take time and energy away from becoming a celebrated actor.

His feelings, however, for Cate were entirely different. She was not a distraction. She was poised to be a true partner supporting and enhancing his journey for fame and fortune as he would for hers.

I've never been this drawn to someone before, his ideas flowed. *I can wait. After all, she's only eighteen years old. Young and inexperienced compared to the women I'm usually with.*

But then his brain hammered back to the frustrating conflict ... the obsession. Her body was perfect, and he had a yearning even thinking about her. This was such strange territory.

Yes, he wanted more, but it was so risky ... *what if I scare her away? What if my intentions are misunderstood? What if my timing's off?*

He had to quiet his nagging mind. Yes, Cate was his friend! But one day ...

Chapter 10
Philosopher "Pi"

Splitting a slice of caramel apple crumble in a small soda shop famous for its tantalizing pastries, Cate and Joseph celebrated his big role in an independent project. Their festivities had been animated and talkative, Cate savoring every moment of the friendly company she would miss with Joseph in New Mexico for a month.

It occurred to her that Kyle would also be traveling, his image plastered across movie billboards as he met with producers discussing future blockbusters.

"So, Joseph, have your lines down?" Cate's straw made a gurgling noise as the last drop of cola was slurped up.

Joseph held up his well-worn script with a boastful gloat. "I do. It's the perfect role for me."

"A psychotic killer?"

"Don't be afraid, *Catherine*," he said in an overly eerie voice. "That's how Oscars are won."

"I'm gonna miss you," she said with a sad guise.

"Wish you had a part in it too. We could pal around after shooting all day." He finished his fountain drink. "So, when are finals?"

"In a few weeks." She folded her napkin neatly and placed it on the table.

"Are you liking your new major?"

Her eyes glinted in approval. "I love philosophy."

"Did I ever tell you that was my favorite subject in college? I almost majored in it. Instead, I ended up in the performing arts. But what I picked up in those classes—common sense beliefs—gave me a roadmap to pursue an acting career."

"Such as?" she asked eagerly.

He scooted his chair closer. "*What goes around comes around.*"

"Ah, karma," she replied astutely. "I agree. Tell me another?"

Sitting back, relaxed, he recited, "*Three things cannot be long hidden: the sun, the moon, and the truth.*"

"Ooh ... Buddha. Deep," she said, enlivened. "This is fun, Joseph. Some more, please."

"Well, I really liked the Native American legends, especially the core belief that everything is connected ... the *Path of Life*."

Cate slid forward, intrigued. "Enlighten, please."

"What, is this a test?" He chuckled, leaning in to match her enthusiasm. "Okay, life's a journey that needs to be lived harmoniously with everything. A give and receive that's balanced. Certain attitudes on the path make up at least part of the twelve tenets of living—respect, humility, cooperation, and being at peace with who you are."

"That's what I love about philosophy. You can pattern yourself after it. I'm fond of *choice, not chance, determines your destiny.*"

"Aristotle. Good one, Ms. Leigh," he acknowledged. "Has that helped your acting career?"

"Not as much as an acting class. But it makes my mental wheels spin, which makes me feel good about myself."

They both laughed heartily, enjoying their intellectual discourse and each other's company.

"You go again," he incited, sitting back.

"Hmm ..."

"How 'bout *living well is the best revenge*?" disrupted a voice from behind.

"George Herbert," Cate retorted, quickly naming the theorist, not realizing who was speaking.

"Kyle, what a surprise," he said tersely. "You coincidentally happened in?"

"You told me this place has great desserts. I had a taste for something sweet." Kyle's gaze landed on Cate, full of warmth. "Hi, Cate," he said, rapt, still struggling to find a balance between his desires and her request for restraint. Playfully, he brushed a crumb from her cheek with his thumb and licked the crumb from his finger. "Mmm, a little caramel. It's good."

Taking her napkin, she wiped her mouth again, blushing.

Joseph glared daggers at his so-called pal. "Shouldn't you be on your way to New York?"

"Tomorrow, like you." Kyle took an unoffered seat beside Cate. "I didn't mean to interrupt your conversation. What were you talking about?"

"We were quoting philosophical principles that we like," she offered. "And we've lived!" Cate laughed, Joseph did not.

"And Kyle's favorite philosophy is hedonism," he snapped. "*What feels good is good.*"

"Funny," Kyle answered coldly as Joseph intensified his disapproving stare.

Placing his arm around the back of Cate's chair was Kyle's not-so-subtle, non-verbal riposte.

She glanced down at her watch. "Oh no, I forgot my brother's taking me to a concert tonight. I have to get home and change."

As she took cash from her purse, they both reached for the check.

"I've got it," insisted Joseph.

Cate tugged harder. "No, my treat this time." She set down the money and stood to go. "Try the apple pie, Kyle. It's delicious. And Joseph, have a great time filming."

She waved with an endearing smile and left.

The two men silently stared at each other.

Finally, Joseph exhaled angrily. "Why are you here, Kyle?"

"I thought I'd stop by and wish you luck." He reached over and patted Joseph on the back.

"We already talked this morning. That's how you knew we were here. You were hoping to see her, weren't you?"

"Is there a problem with that?"

Kyle was not ready to tell Joseph he'd been spending time with Cate.

"Yes, Kyle, she's my friend."

"She can't have more than one friend?"

"No," Joseph blurted and then, looking about the place, continued, lowering his voice, "I know what you're after. Talk about a soul not in harmony with life."

"You're wrong."

"Am I?!"

After a long pause, Kyle, with a forced smile, stuck out his hand to shake his oldest friend's. "Have a good shoot."

"Thanks."

Leaving Kyle to his thoughts, Joseph walked out into the late afternoon.

Chapter 11
City of Diablo

It was a week later, on a bright, clear Sunday morning. The knock came unexpectedly. Cate peered out the peephole. Her college theater instructor?

Cracking the door open, she probed, "Mr. Greco, is something wrong?"

"Catherine, I want to speak with you." He stepped forward, his presence affronting.

"Well, couldn't we talk after class tomorrow?" she asked guardedly.

"I came over here as it's vital to review today. May I come in?" He pushed his hand onto the door.

"Um, I guess so."

Slowly opening the door, she was pushed back as Greco forced it open and slammed it behind him. Cate instantly realized this was a big mistake. Wandering throughout her living room, his creepy vibe intensified as he picked up photos of her family.

"Who's this?" He gripped the picture of Edward. "Your boyfriend?"

"My brother." Staying pressed against the door, she did not venture any closer.

Greco traversed to her sofa and rested comfortably on it.

"Catherine, come over here. We need to discuss your acting abilities," he said with an intimidating tenor.

"My abilities?" Doubtfully, she walked to the sofa and sat in the furthest corner.

"How old are you?" He threw his arm across the back of the sofa, extending toward her.

She squashed herself even further away from him.

"I'll be nineteen in a couple of weeks."

"Nineteen? You're not even of drinking age."

Finding the statement off-putting, she floundered. "I don't drink. I prefer ginger ale."

"Spiked?" he taunted.

"Ah, no." She tensely exhaled. "Mr. Greco, what did you want to say?"

"You're of Italian descent, aren't you? I can tell." His leer burrowed through her.

"Yes."

The hair on the back of her neck bristled, and his ogle made her feel like she was being undressed.

"I, too, was raised very traditionally. I understand what being reared by strict religious parents means. Old fashioned restrictions."

With secret dread, Cate silently prayed for help.

"Your point, sir, is?"

Kyle approached Cate's apartment, ready to knock on her door. He could hear a man's gruff voice inside and Cate's response.

The inner daytime curtains were closed, allowing diffused light to seep into the apartment. Kyle stepped closer to the window to listen, remaining out of sight. Although no one inside could see him, there was a slight separation between the curtains, and he could make out the two sitting on the sofa—Greco, brash and menacing at one end, and Cate, disoriented and stiff at the other.

"As we have examined in class, you're a fine actress but holding back. No matter my instructions, it appears you're having difficulty letting go. I've concluded it's the old-fashioned traditions you were reared to believe. They're not suitable today, and you're limiting yourself as a performer. So, even though it'll be a lot of additional effort on my part, I've elected your talent's worth the extra work to help relieve you of your family's burden and their antiquated moral structure."

Puzzled, her voice squeaked loudly, "You wanna do what?"

"After class, I'd be willing to come over here and personally tutor you. We'll begin slowly to help you grow as a woman. I do mean, take our time. First, we'd merely lay in bed together naked …"

Cate leaped up, swiftly backing toward the door, her hands reaching for the doorknob.

"Mr. Greco, you have to leave," she bawled.

"Catherine, it may sound unconventional. I assure you it'll be pleasurable. We could begin today." He walked deliberately toward her.

Fumbling to turn the doorknob behind her, she never took her sight off him. "You need to go now!"

⚜

Kyle knew he had to intervene and hurriedly tried the doorknob, but it was locked. Suddenly, the door flew open. Cate, running backward without looking, fell into his arms. She turned her head to see who had caught her. Her terrified expression implored him.

He gave Greco a deadly scowl. "Everything all right, Cate?"

Without a word, the theater coach slipped past the two, Kyle's stare not losing its intensity.

Leading her in, Kyle closed the door behind them. He turned

her around and held her vision. "Did he hurt you?"
Her breathing was shallow from fear, and she was on the verge of hyperventilating.
"Slow down your breathing," he encouraged. She toiled to breathe out, appearing to have forgotten how. Pulling her into an embrace, he felt her shaking.
"It's okay," he said, taking a slow, deep breath to demonstrate, attempting to get her to follow his example. "Breathe with me. I'm here." He held her until she calmed down, never feeling so strongly the need to protect someone.
I should've decked that bastard the minute Cate opened the door, he thought.
She spoke faintly, "I was praying for help. That was so scary. Thank you, Kyle, for being here, for saving me."
Pulling her close again, Cate rested her muddled head on his shoulder. Suddenly, she gently pushed him away.
"Wait, why are you here?"
Kyle searched her deep brown eyes. "You see, I got home late yesterday, and I thought you might like to ride to Costa Mesa with me to meet my grandmother. She watches Pepper when I'm away. Plus, I check on her when I can. And then we could get some dinner on the coast. It'd be nice to have company on the long drive."
Taking a calming breath, she felt the weight of terror lift from her as she processed his request. "Yes, please, I would love to. Thank you. Would you please excuse me for a minute to change my clothes?"
Edna was correct. Cate was perhaps the most polite and appreciative girl he'd ever met.
"Sure, I'll wait here."
She stopped and faced him to gaze into his eyes, emphasizing her immense gratitude. "Thank you."

She remained a little aloof, fighting the disturbing images of Greco. Kyle sought to cheer her up. He flipped on the FM radio and played Cheap Trick's *I Want You to Want Me*.

"Memory?" he began.

"Last week at Universal Amphitheater. My brother took me." She smiled at the recollection.

"No, no! Not an old enough memory. You just went to that concert. That's not how the game's played," he teased.

"So you're making the rules of the game I created," she laughed. "What's yours?"

He side-glanced her. "You really wanna know?"

"Isn't that the goal of the game?"

"The back seat of my old car on prom night."

"Okay, stop," she flushed. "Already too much information."

"I warned you what most songs remind me of." He immediately began to sing again.

Oh, didn't I, didn't I, didn't I see you cryin' ...

Cate smoothly harmonized with him, thrilled with her newfound confidence. Being with Kyle made her happy.

The car stopped in front of a quaint residence in the suburbs of Costa Mesa.

"This is your grandmother's?" she asked. "You're lucky. All my grandparents have passed."

The door opened, and a stately, graceful woman, seventy years of age, stepped out, holding Pepper in her arms.

Kyle hollered, "Hey, Nana." He gave her a big hug and kiss on the cheek.

"My sweet boy, what a surprise! And who is this lovely girl?"

"My friend Cate. Cate, this is Nana, my grandmother."

Opening her arms wide, Cate gave Nana a warm hug. "So nice to meet you."

And they entered a world of colorful perennials and the delicious smell of cake baking.

Cate beheld the beauty. "What incredible flowers!"

"They're from my garden. Come with me, dear." Taking Cate by the hand, Nana led her outside.

The backyard was full of beds of vibrant flowers in bloom. The aroma was striking to the senses. Nana and Cate sat on a bench while Kyle sat on the border of the bricked-raised bed of lavender, playing with Pepper.

They talked for more than an hour, Nana sharing the details of her life with her grandson. Cate heard about a tragic car accident in which his parents were killed when he was eight. There were no other relatives except his grandmother to care for the boy. She gushed with pride at what a wonderful young man he had become and how well he was doing in his acting career.

Watching Kyle diffidently accept the compliments with a schoolboy charm, Cate thought what a sad, lonely childhood he had had, causing her to view him differently.

He was nothing like the scoundrel the tabloids painted. Certainly, he didn't take every girl he knew to meet his grandmother, she determined. No, he was so thoughtful and generous. A genuinely nice man and a loving grandson. Noticing his face alight with affection and humility as he listened to his grandmother brag about him, she hit upon the truth—this was the real Kyle.

When it was time to depart, Nana held Cate for a long moment. For a second, the threat of what happened earlier dissolved within this cordial, welcoming home. She felt secure here. Nana was drawn to Cate's sweet spirit and stroked her face as if saying goodbye to a grandchild.

Walking to the car, Pepper by her side, Cate gave Kyle a few minutes alone with his grandmother.

"I'll stop by next week and pick up Pepper." He hugged her, and Nana gripped his hand to keep him from leaving.

"What're you doing with that nice girl?" she quietly demanded. "She's the first girl you've brought home since you moved to Los Angeles."

"What do you mean what am I doing?"

"Kyle Weston, she's a good girl. She's the kind of girl you marry, not toy with. So, what are your intentions with that dear girl?"

"She's a friend," he said defensively.

"I hope so." She wagged her finger at him. "Don't hurt her."

"Nana, you sound like Joseph. I'm not a villain."

"Of course you're not a villain. Never could be. You're just a naughty boy." She patted his cheek.

He laughed, "I love you, Nana."

Giving him a big hug, she looked him straight in the eye. "And I love you, too."

He kissed her cheek and headed to the car.

"Hey, little guy." Picking up Pepper, Kyle snuggled him as he walked back to Nana. "You're gonna stay with Nana for a little longer, okay?" Once again, he kissed his grandmother as he handed her Pepper. "Thanks for everything, Nana. Love you."

～

As they drove up the coast, Cate flashed an effervescent smile.

"You're grandmother's wonderful!"

"Guess what? She thinks you're really special, too."

Chapter 12
San Diego

Doris's kitchen smelled of bubbling Italian sauce made from scratch, the scent of spices and herbs blending with the ocean's cool breeze a block from their home.

"Catherine, it's so wonderful having you and your brother home. How's living in the big city?" Doris stirred powdered garlic into the large pot of sauce.

"It's fine, Mom. I miss you and my friends. Have you seen any of them?" Helping her mom cook, Cate handed her salt and pepper. "Tommy or Roger? Have they stopped by?"

"No, dear, not Roger. I heard Tommy returned to Connecticut to be with his folks."

"I miss them. They were the best buddies."

"Yes, they're nice young men." Turning down the flame on the gas range, Doris wiped her hands. "How's school?"

"I changed my major to philosophy." Cate hopped up on the counter to take a seat. "It's a core subject. I'll graduate a year early."

Sounding disappointed, her mom bemoaned, "Oh, honey, I loved attending your cute productions."

"I know, but I haven't given up acting. I changed when one of my teachers came on to me. It was impossible to stay in his class. I had to drop it. Unfortunately, it was a prerequisite course for theater. It threw me a year behind. It's fine. Philosophy's inspiring. I especially love Aristotle." Recalling her quotation exchange with Joseph, Cate theatrically presented, "*Quality is not an act. It is a habit.*"

"Honey, you're so intelligent," she said with pride. "So, have you made any friends up there?"

"Yes, a couple of great ones."

Edward entered the kitchen to hang up the cordless phone, hearing his sister's statement.

Retrieving a soup spoon from the drawer, Doris dipped it into the sauce and held it to Cate's mouth. "Taste. What does it need?"

Sampling a small amount from the spoon, Cate mulled, "Hmm, more oregano?"

As she finished what her daughter left on the spoon, Doris nodded, "You're right. Yes, oregano."

Sliding off the countertop, Cate turned her attention to her brother. "How's Valerie?"

"Fine."

"Can't you be without her for one minute? Is she afraid you might have a life other than hers?"

"Catherine. Stop that. It's your brother's choice," Doris lectured, adding the oregano to the sauce.

"She's so manipulative!"

"Catherine. None of your business," her mom scolded.

"Okay, Mom." Cate opened the refrigerator, foraging for a cool drink.

"Edward, frankly, I'm not fond of her either," she admitted. "Catherine has a point. She doesn't treat you well."

"See," Cate preened.

Edward stared at them, perturbed. "Both of you back off. She's my girlfriend. You don't have to like her. I do." Breaking off a piece of fresh Italian bread, he dipped it in the sauce to try it. "And weren't we discussing Catherine's new L.A. friends?"

"They're not new. I met Joseph a couple of months after I moved there. We've been friends for nearly a year. He's in my acting class." She grabbed a bottle of ginger ale. "We were partnered up from the beginning."

"First I've heard of it. What does 'partnered up' mean?" He looked at her suspiciously.

"Acting partners," Cate sparred. "Geez."

"You mentioned a couple, darling?" Doris continued to stir the contents of the large pot.

"Yeah, and a friend of Joseph's. Kyle Weston."

Edward was ruffled. "Wait. The movie star?!"

"He's not a movie star." She pondered, "Well, not yet. He's getting there."

"Mom, have you heard of Kyle Weston?" submitted Edward bitingly.

"Yes, of course. He's rather good-looking." Their mom then sprinkled some more parsley into the sauce.

"See, if our reclusive mother has heard of him, he's famous," he said cockily, impressed with himself for making a lawyer-type case.

"I'm not reclusive. I don't have much energy to socialize these days."

"I can relate," blustered Cate.

Doris slapped her son's hand as he tried to dip more bread into the pot. "Enough, Edward! You'll spoil your appetite."

"What?! I'm trying the sauce for you," he protested. "Needs salt."

Testing it again, she balked, "It does not."

"Let's get back to this Weston issue," he garbled, stuffing the bread into his mouth.

"What issue?"

"He has his picture taken with a million actresses and models. How do you fit in, Miss Dense?" He poured some water to wash down the bread he'd been eating.

"I beg your pardon." Cate was offended. "What's that supposed to mean?"

"Oh my! Isn't the world so nice and giggly," he said snippily.

Doris put her hands on her hips and chided, "The only reason I allowed Catherine to move up there was you were to keep an eye on her, Edward, as your father told you."

"It's a full-time job looking out for her, Mom," he droned. "And I have my own life."

"I never asked you to," Cate grumbled.

"You're serious?!" Edward mockingly imitated his sister in a high-pitched voice, "Ed, please talk to my landlord and have him fix the shower. I don't have any hot water. I'm scared to talk to the big bad landlord. Oh, and the air-conditioning broke. It stinks in here."

Cate sneered at him. "You can be so mean."

"Both of you are driving me crazy," sighed Doris. "Catherine, tell me, dear, about your friend Kyle."

"We have acting in common." She sat at the kitchen table.

"He's not just an actor," Edward snarled, "he's a celebrity."

"As a matter of fact, he asked me to go to the premiere of *Will-Maker* with him," she boasted.

"Oh no! You're not going." Her brother stood over her chair. "That's not a date. It's an invitation to get laid!"

"Edward!" both women shouted over the other.

"Hey, you insist I watch out for her. That's me taking care of my sister." He strolled to the loaf of bread and eyed it. "Think about it, Catherine. A premiere of a major motion picture with a celebrity wolfhound."

"I don't believe that."

"Some guys are much smoother than rockers hitting on you thinking you're a groupie. And I'm not there to protect you."

"Mom?" she appealed to her mother, who shrugged and returned to stirring the sauce.

Gavrihel

"Your brother might be right, Catherine. A premiere's a major event."

"Neither one of you knows him. It's so unfair to judge someone you've never even met. He's truly kind."

"Maybe so. But it doesn't mean sex isn't in his playbook." He checked to see if his mother wasn't looking and peeled off some crust of the Italian bread and ate it.

Cate turned up her nose. "Fine, don't men constantly think of sex anyway?"

"Not about my sister," he mangled while munching on the bread.

"He's a friend," she whined.

"Honey, listen to your brother. I don't want to have to bring you back home. But if something happens to you, I will. I'm still your mother."

She squinted at her brother's stern glare and her mother's worried bearing. "Okay, I won't go." Turning on her heels, she stomped out the kitchen door to sit on the old swing set and pouted.

Doris backhanded Edward's arm hard.

"Hey!" he yelped.

"You're supposed to be watching out for her! Stop being so wrapped up in your own love life! And Catherine's right—Valerie's not good for you. So, quit thinking about what's between your legs and use your brain instead," she tapped her son's forehead. "Meet a nice girl already!"

Chapter 13
Beer and Corn Nuts

"Welcome home. How was the shoot?" Kyle had ordered Joseph a beer, waiting for his arrival in their usual watering hole.

Taking his seat, Joseph was ready to unwind. "It was fine. How's the publicity tour doing?"

"It hasn't ramped up yet." Kyle set the extra beer in front of Joseph. "So, Joseph, did you fall in love with anybody in New Mexico?"

"No, too focused on my role." He poured the beer into the frosted mug. "How 'bout you, Kyle? Did you ever snag someone to go to the premiere with you?"

"I did. Unfortunately, she backed out."

"You're losing your touch," he razzed, hoisting his glass to drink.

"No, that wasn't on my mind at all." The corners of Kyle's mouth turned up into a satisfied grin. "She's different, in the best way."

"Who exactly are we talking about?"

"Cate, of course."

"Kyle, I told you to leave her alone." He slammed down the mug.

"It's not what you think. We're friends, that's all. I swear."

Sitting back, arms crossed, Joseph glared at Kyle. "And you invited your *friend* to go to a premiere? A one-way ticket to your bed."

Gavrihel

"As I said, she's a friend and no one-way ticket. I reasoned it might be fun to share the big event with her instead of someone I may not see again past a date or two."
"But the good news is Cate turned you down!"
"She changed her mind," he corrected. "Although she sounded bummed about it."
"The girl's savvier than I thought. She knows your end game."
"That's not true." Kyle sat back, holding his beer bottle.
"I hope so."
"You're a lousy wingman, ya know that?" he said glibly, shaking his head.
Snacking on the corn nut mix in the bowl at the center of the table, Joseph goaded, "I've never been your wingman, but I am your oldest friend. And I'd like to keep you walking the straight and narrow. So, who are you gonna take now?"
"The other day, I met an actress, Sophie—I don't remember her last name. My agent introduced us, and we had lunch. Well, we never quite made it to lunch."
"Typical," he said with a rank of admiration. "Tell me, was she any good?"
Kyle didn't respond. Directly thinking about Cate, guilt ensnared his mind.
Joseph studied his pal's far-off look. "What?"
Kyle shook his head.
"Fine, you have a replacement date for the premiere then?" Joseph motioned to the waitress to get two more beers.
He shrugged. "If we last long enough."
"You can always bring me. Not going to bed with you, though," chuckled Joseph.
"Not my type," laughed Kyle.

Changing the subject to Kyle's next project to begin filming in October, the afternoon passed. Joseph left to unpack, leaving him alone at the bar. Beer in hand, he sloped down on the jukebox, perusing to hit upon a tune to match his mood. He chose Led Zeppelin's *In the Evening* and stared at the colorful lights highlighting the record. He saw a pay phone and stepped over to pick up the receiver, dropping a coin in to dial Cate.

"Hello, Cate. How are you?"

"Fine. How're you today?" She had the jolliest quality in her voice.

"Good. Cate, may I ask you a question? Please be honest. Why did you change your mind about attending the premiere with me?"

Sinking onto the sofa, she rifled for a credible reason since she desperately wanted to go. "My family had concerns."

"What do you mean? Do you?"

"No!" she replied speedily. "I totally trust you."

He held a long breath.

Cate felt restless in the silence. "Kyle? Don't be mad, please."

"I'm not mad," he said ruefully. "I'm disappointed because I wanted to share it with you."

"I told my family they didn't know you. If they did, they'd never imagine you're some sort of scoundrel," she defended. "My brother called you a wolfdog ... or something like that."

"No, they're wise to be protective of you. I feel the same way." He paused. "Hey, why don't I meet your brother sometime?"

She scrunched her face in disapproval. "Um, not a good idea."

"Why? Are you ashamed of me?"

"No, he takes his role as Italian big brother too seriously."

"You're only half Italian."

"Tell *him* that," she laughed.

"So, what're you doing tonight? I missed your birthday. I owe you a movie. What do you say?"

Excitement lifted her voice. "Yes. Where should we meet?"

"Grauman's. Have you seen the newest *Back to the Future*?"

"It's not out yet. It opens Memorial Day weekend, the same day as your film. I've been to most of the new releases this year."

With a slight timbre of jealousy, he asked, "Who've you gone with?"

"No one. I go alone."

Her usual process surprised him.

"Except I haven't seen *Pretty Woman*," she added.

"Neither have I. Okay, meet you there."

Chapter 14
Italian Brother

The concert hall was packed with Bon Jovi fans—the exuberance and anticipation of the show energized the arena. Edward had procured excellent tickets. Interning at one of the West Coast's biggest entertainment law firms had its benefits.

"Thank you for doing this," she grinned. "Getting seats for my friends, I mean."

"I'd expect Kyle Weston could get his own ticket to a concert."

"Ed, please be nice. Joseph and Kyle are my dearest friends. I want your approval."

Her brother snorted, maddened. "My approval? If you wanted that, you'd live with Mom, not in this sleazy town."

Joseph and Kyle shimmied by the other fans in the first few chairs to get to Cate and her brother. They shook Edward's hand.

"Ed, these are my friends Joseph Beason and Kyle Weston."

"Thank you for inviting us," Kyle said. "Great seats."

"No problem," he whisked.

Kyle asked, "Your law firm represents the groups you see?"

"Yeah, either currently or hopefully in the future. Entertainment law's similar to acting. You have to 'audition' for the job."

"Don't take offense, but why do you bring your sister to concerts, not a girlfriend?" quizzed Joseph.

"My firm expects us to be professional, no dates. Spouses are different. It's brilliant bringing Catherine. The established rock bands are family men and love that she's my kid sister. They remember me, great for business relations."

"I'm a prop," Cate cajoled.

"A lovely prop," admired Kyle.

Agitated, Edward stared.

"Excuse me," she said, "I'm finding the ladies' room before the concert begins." She glided past Edward and left the other side of the row.

"So," Edward faced the two men, "you guys are her friends, huh? Do know, I love my little sister. And as far as I'm concerned, it's stupid that she's even in Los Angeles. I constantly worry she's in this business. Too many vultures."

"We agree," said Joseph with an easy-going tone.

Her brother strained an amiable countenance. "I'll get to the point." He stared directly at Kyle and only at him. "I don't care who you are. If you ever hurt my sister, I'll beat the living hell out of you. Are we clear?"

"Crystal," muttered Joseph.

"Understood." Kyle nodded, suppressing his smile.

"Good," he said, shaking his head to lighten up. "I should caution you, Catherine loves concerts."

"What do you mean?" asked Joseph.

"You'll see," he chuckled.

The lights dimmed as Cate scooted down the row, and her brother let her by to get to her seat.

Kyle murmured in her ear, "I like your brother."

∞

Yes, Cate unconditionally loved concerts. And Bon Jovi was one of her favorite bands. She was out of her seat for most of the show, jumping up and down excitedly, singing at the top of her lungs, in harmony with the rest of the audience. Kyle noted she was no longer bashful about singing in public, at least not here. The three chuckled at her, lost in the live performance, transported and childlike.

Edward stretched to the guys across her empty seat. "See what I mean. Crazy about concerts."

Her two friends knew she loved movies. Here, however, was a whole new level of zeal.

When Bon Jovi sang *Lay Your Hands on Me*, Cate bobbed to the music, Kyle slid up in his seat and smiled at her. Then he saw Edward eying them.

If you want me to lay my hands on you ...
Lay your hands on me, lay your hands on me ...

Edward looked at his sister, then scowled directly at the *wolfhound*, giving a very slight angry shake of his head. Kyle instantly got the message and sat back.

A few songs later, *Livin' on a Prayer* began. Cate was ecstatic, again jumping up and belting out the tune.

Joseph yanked Kyle over to him and, in hushed tones, warned, "Stop staring at her ass."

"What?" he uttered, stymied. "I'm not."

"Oh yes, you are," scoffed Joseph. "You're ogling!"

"Joseph, she's standing in front of me, bouncing up and down. It's tough not to stare. She's adorable."

"Well, you better stop. Her brother's about to haul off and punch you in the nose ... deservedly."

Sure enough, Edward had one eye on the stage and one on him. Heeding his pal's advice, Kyle stood up beside Cate, joining in on the song enlisting her enthusiasm and charm. As usual, he was enchanted.

∽∾

The highlight of the evening for Cate was to venture backstage with Edward to meet the bands. Flashing their security clearance and avoiding the bustle of roadies dismantling and moving equipment out to the large eighteen-wheelers for the next show, the four made their way into the area where the opening act, WeSheim, was entertaining their fans before heading to the reception area for the headliners, Bon Jovi, who were an example, as Edward had said, of nice established family men.

The four weaved their way through WeSheim's unruly fan base, heading further into the gathering. Despite Kyle's rising celebrity status, the music fans were mainly enamored with WeSheim, not paying him any mind. However, an occasional female would screech in excitement, trying to grab his arm while Kyle smiled politely and kept moving forward, Joseph aiding in blocking the attempts.

As they turned a corner, having fallen slightly behind, Cate was unexpectedly culled from her group. Digger Waller, WeSheim's lead singer, sidelined her. Lusting at her beauty, he aggressively backed her into a corner. Cate's eyes searched for her brother, realizing she was on her own in her predicament.

When they entered Bon Jovi's reception area, Kyle turned around, noticing Cate wasn't with them.

"Where's Cate?" he asked no one in particular, swiftly walking back around the corner to where WeSheim and their fans were partying. Edward also became aware his sister wasn't with them.

Through the packed room, Kyle was staggered to see Digger trying to force Cate to kiss him as she actively avoided his mouth. Digger paused to say something in her ear; a darting look of outrage shaded her face.

Both Kyle and Edward saw her cock her fist and punch Digger as hard as she could in his stomach. He doubled over in pain.

Although Kyle's anger rose as he rushed to confront the bastard, he still marveled at Cate's grit as she ran to her brother.

With a pasted smile, he crouched before Digger to see his face twisted in pain. "So, Waller," he smirked, "quite a wallop from such a petite girl."

Digger struggled to respond, only moaning.

In a low, threatening voice, Kyle commanded, "Never go near her again, hear me?"

Clutching his abdomen while laboring to catch his breath, Digger growled snidely, "Are you takin' a piss, movie star?! Like you've never asked for a hummer from a piece of ass!"

Enraged, Kyle slugged Digger in the jaw without thinking. Furiously, he raised his fists to take another swing when Joseph yanked Kyle away, dragging him to the side where Edward and Cate waited, her hand covering her mouth in shock at what she was witnessing.

A few fans and mates hurried to assist Digger.

As Cate rubbed Kyle's back soothingly, Edward directed Joseph, "Get them out of here before word gets out what happened. Go out the back way." He grabbed Joseph's arm. "And Joseph, no matter what, don't let the paparazzi get a photo of them, especially my sister."

"What're you gonna do?"

"I'll handle this. Now go."

The three exited and carefully went through the loading dock to the parking area without incident.

Collapsing in the backseat, Kyle slumped down, confounded by his impulsive reaction to shield this sweet girl.

Humbled, Cate looked at him from the passenger seat. "Kyle, I'm so sorry. But thank you."

He glanced up at her, surprised. "Why are you sorry, Cate? It wasn't your fault. I just …"

"Ed'll take care of it," she hastily assured. "He's good at what he does."

"I may have to hire him full-time." He broke a meek smile and reclined, closing his eyes.

Cate leaned close to Joseph, his eyes fixed on the road ahead.
"He didn't have to do that," she whispered.
"Yeah, he did."

∞

The fracas made the front page of the insidious *Movie Inquiry Magazine*. Fascinated by the scene beginning with Digger groping Cate, a fan snapped the moment of impact and sold it to the tabloid for a tidy sum. The headline read: "*Wanker or Wonder?*"

There were two diverse versions of the story making the rounds. One of insane jealousy because Digger hit on the movie star's new girlfriend and one more accurate tale of an arrogant rocker forcing himself upon a young girl and Kyle interceding to defend her. Despite Kyle's roguish reputation, his measured temperament and gentlemanly ways were well-known and appreciated. So, the latter story overtook the pages. In fact, there appeared to be a legion of Kyle's admirers who thought his protective nature was praiseworthy.

Over the next few weeks, Digger's popularity rose from the onslaught of publicity. WeSheim's newest single, a tale of seduction gone wrong, *Punk Rubbish*, went to number one on the *Billboard Charts*. After the musical success and enhancement of his rebel bravado, Digger was pleased. This enabled Edward to easily convince the tough, working-class Brit to not pursue a civil case against Kyle since his little sister had initially bested him ... and that would be a blow to his misogynistic ego.

Perhaps the most favorable outcome was that Edward was more approving of Kyle's comradery with his kid sister.

Chapter 15
Rhythm of the Night

The nightclub had a large dance floor surrounded by tabletops and stools. The sound booth was off to the side, the DJ spinning *Vogue* by Madonna.

"You can't drink, ya know," alerted Joseph. "It was hard enough getting you in here being underage. I don't want Trent to get in trouble for allowing you in."

"I wasn't planning to. I don't like drinking," Cate discounted. "Except I love champagne. My family has it on the holidays."

"Expensive taste," he remarked and saw Kyle walking in with an attractive woman his age, with shoulder-length blond hair and intense green eyes.

"Hi, guys," called Kyle. "This is Julia Morris. Julia, these are my friends, Cate and Joseph. Julia and I went to high school together."

"Hi," they greeted in unison.

"I've heard a lot about you both," Julia said.

"Julia, so you went with Kyle to the premiere. How was it?" Joseph began a conversation.

"It was fabulous. Great first date after being apart for six years," said Julia happily.

Cate subtly turned away.

Noticing, Kyle changed the subject. "Going dancing was Julia's idea."

"Kyle told me he had to learn for his acting career. I wanted to see if there was any improvement from the senior prom when he was trouncing my toes."

Everyone snickered.

They discovered Julia had accepted a job at one of the studio's accounting departments, becoming acclimated to her move to the big city.

The two women would instantly connect. Julia was generous in spirit, and Cate found her to be a quality person with common interests. It was apparent the ladies were getting along quite well.

Joseph whispered to Kyle that he'd never seen Cate relate to other girls, especially the other actresses in the class. She didn't make many female friends.

***

When the music kicked into high gear, Cate towed Joseph out to dance. Stiffly, he followed Cate's smooth lead as she showed him different steps and fun moves. Kyle and Julia watched.

"Cate, you're good," Julia cheered as they returned to the table.

"My mom was a professional ballroom dancer. She taught me."

"Did she do exhibition dancing?"

"Yeah, she was phenomenal," she said proudly.

"Where do your folks live?"

"Mom lives in San Diego." Solemnly, she relayed, "My dad passed away a few years ago. Heart attack."

"I didn't know. I'm sorry," Kyle said kindheartedly.

She forced a smile, and his empathetic gaze arrested her sad eyes.

Julia perceived the bond between them.

With her purse in hand, Julia urged, "Cate, I'm finding the powder room. Join me?"

"Sure."

The two strolled away.

"That's so bizzare," declared Joseph. "Why do women do that?" He exaggeratedly acted in a high-pitched voice, "Oh Kyle, can we go to the powder room together? You can keep me company because I hate to piss alone."

They laughed, and Joseph moved over to Cate's empty chair to speak privately. "Since when do you introduce your friends to your new girlfriend? Isn't it a waste of time? How long'll this one last?"

"No, Julia's not a girlfriend. I don't have girlfriends, remember? She's a friend. And I made it clear I wasn't in the market to start a relationship or exclusivity."

"What a waste of a premiere ticket. A friend. So, you didn't get laid?"

"Yeah, we had sex," Kyle answered nonchalantly.

His pal sighed, irked. "Hey, I have big news. Guess where I was last week while you were on the East Coast promoting your film? Playboy Mansion!"

"No shit!" Kyle's interest was piqued. "How did you end up there?"

"Cate," he raised his eyebrows.

"Cate?!"

"Yeah, she was at an audition at Universal. A scout for the magazine was walking the lot for some interesting areas to shoot a cover and spotted her. He gave her his card and invited her to the mansion that night to meet Hefner. She wasn't going alone, so I accompanied her. Man, the place's everything you imagine." He looked upward, enthralled.

"Wait," Kyle started jumpily. "Hold it. She's not …"

"Oh no, of course not! That'd be way too J. Geils' *Centerfold*," he laughed. "No, she met with Heff. She said he was a gentleman, all business. He said he wanted her to test for Miss March. He told her there was big money in being a centerfold. Cate answered, *no, thank you*, because her grandmother might see her."

Kyle moved discreetly forward. "She told me her grandparents were dead."

"Kyle, it was an excuse."

"Yeah, Cate would never …"

"Nah. I'm glad I went with her, though," he sighed deeply, enjoying the memory. "I met some influential people and a hot bunny."

"Did you hook up?" asked Kyle with an impish grin.

"No, I had to make sure Cate got home safely. The bunny and I have a date next Saturday night. You know, having Cate around has some real benefits."

Kyle scowled at him.

"Not those kinds of benefits." Joseph jerked his head. "Like a sister, remember? She's a magnet for opportunities in this business."

※

Julia stood at the mirror freshening her lipstick while Cate washed her hands.

"Kyle's simply a friend," informed Julia.

The revelation unsettled Cate.

"I'm not saying I wouldn't like it to be more, but he's obsessed with success and becoming a celebrity. Ya know what I mean?"

"No, not really," frowned Cate. "I don't see him that way."

"If I needed him," she said, fixing her hair, "he'd never drop everything to be by my side. When we were younger, he was attentive. Now, he's centered on his career, and all else's secondary to him."

Cate doubted Julia was as ambiguous toward Kyle as she tried to project. Perhaps she was protecting her heart. If the roles were reversed, Cate knew how she'd feel …

"Girls everywhere. Nothing serious," Julia continued. "He

discourages the women he's dating from visiting him on location. He's focused on his performance. Or maybe it's due to the fact he's sleeping with a gal working on the shoot with him," she scorned, staring into the mirror. "It's understandable. He's a rising star. Anyway, that's why we're friends and nothing more. How 'bout you? Any boyfriends?"

"No, I don't have time to date," replied Cate inelegantly.

Julia studied her dubiously. "You've had a boyfriend, haven't you?"

"I … um … have a lot of guy friends. All my life. Like Kyle and Joseph."

Checking out the restroom to ensure they were alone, Julia stepped closer to her. "May I ask you something personal?"

"Okay," she said cautiously.

"Are you a virgin?"

"Ahh …" Cate froze. She didn't expect Julia to be invasively direct.

"Not a difficult question. Yes or no? Have you ever been with a guy?"

"No," she squeaked in discomfort.

"No, you're not a virgin?" persisted Julia. "Or, no, you are?"

"I've never been with anyone," she answered warily.

Julia put the comb in her handbag. "I knew it."

Cate was flushed red with embarrassment. "Do you … do you think anyone else knows?"

"If by anyone else you mean Kyle and Joseph … ah, yes. It's fairly obvious." Facing Cate with hands on her hips, she spouted, "What the hell are you doing in Hollywood? The worst place in the world for being naïve."

"I'm not." Cate felt slighted.

Julia stared at her disbelievingly.

"Okay," she cowered, "but I'm not jaded."

"Far from it," Julia said. "You need someone to explain the

world to you before you get hurt. A trustworthy friend who'll watch out for you."

"I have Joseph and Kyle."

"They're guys. I mean, a female friend who's got your back."

"I don't have any female friends."

Merrily, Julia offered, "Neither do I. Wanna hang out sometime?"

"That'd be fun," Cate said enthusiastically as Julia looped her arm around her new friend's.

Together, they set out of the restroom. She tugged on Julia's arm, stopping her before she exited. "Julia, you won't say anything, will you?"

"Oh, Cate." Julia shook her head.

∞

When the girls approached the table, the DJ played a record with a Latin beat. Kyle invited Julia to dance.

"No, thank you. I can't do that. Ask Cate. I bet she can."

"Cate?" He extended his hand.

"Sure."

They flowed with the rhythm gracefully. Their actions were smooth, anticipating every move like they had been in each other's arms for years.

When they returned to their seats, Julia was impressed. "Do that again," she ordered.

"What?" Kyle was baffled.

"You two were incredible. Weren't they, Joseph?"

Joseph nodded, preoccupied. An attractive woman on the other side of the bar was making eyes at him.

"Seriously, go dance again," she insisted, applauding her support.

Kyle gladly reached for Cate's hand and spun her into a waltz.

The group danced late into the night, with Joseph wandering over to chat with the lady wooing him. And although Julia twirled around the floor with Kyle once or twice, he spent most of the evening dancing with Cate … with Julia's approval.

"You two should go into competition," she bragged.

It was true. The more they danced together, the more proficient they became.

Finally, they all rose to leave.

"So, Kyle's filming in town the next couple of weeks," Julia began. "Maybe we can all plan another get-together."

"That'd be fun," said Cate brightly.

"It's too bad," Joseph absentmindedly undertook, "you've not been on a film set yet, Cate, even to just watch the process."

"Good idea," said Kyle, his face vivifying with elation. "Cate, why don't you come by the soundstage next week. It's a closed set, but I'll put your name on the list."

"I didn't mean …" Joseph stuttered.

Cate glanced worriedly at Julia, not wanting to upset her new friend.

Kyle and Julia left together, and Joseph drove Cate to her apartment, abruptly saying goodnight. He was meeting up later with the woman from the bar.

Chapter 16
Movie Star

A week passed, and Cate found herself in the waiting area of a production office on the grounds of a major film studio. There was an enchantment about driving onto the lot and winding her way to the back offices to read for a role.

The receptionist at the desk, keeping the hopefuls in order, was reading the latest tabloid. Plastered on the front page was a photo of Kyle and his current costar entering a restaurant. The woman closed the magazine and noticed Cate angling her head to read the headline.

"Isn't he dreamy?" she swooned.

Cate nodded, a bit red-faced.

Looking around the room to make sure she could speak confidentially, the receptionist said, "Being in this job, I've met a lot of famous men who end up being real jerks. But Kyle Weston … I certainly would hop into his bed in a heartbeat! Mmm-mmm," she giggled. "Would you like to look at it? I'm finished, and frankly, my boss gets ticked off that I'm reading it." She held out the paper to Cate. "Here, you can keep it."

Cate smiled, "Thanks."

As she paged through, a disgruntled expression crossed her face at each photo of Kyle and the woman, her heart sinking. She had to remind herself he was not her boyfriend. How could he be? He was a handsome star with glamorous, available women

Plating Magic Hour

hanging all over him. When it came to attraction, she was definitely out of his league.

She glimpsed at the mirror on the wall. She looked so young and sweet. She might as well have a halo over her head. No wonder all the parts she was sent out on were high school girls. Always the comic relief, never the love interest or sexy siren.

Gazing at Kyle's eyes, she felt a longing.

"Catherine Leigh," a voice called at the opened door leading to the purpose of her visit—landing the role. She quickly folded the magazine, stuffing it into her purse.

Leaving the audition, feeling as she always did, a little off-balanced and not as confident as she should, Cate decided to roam the area, taking advantage of being on a film lot. Halting sharply, she saw the soundstage where *Tattersail*, Kyle's production, was being filmed. Initially, she had decided, when he invited her to stop by, not to go. But this seemed awfully fortuitous.

Already dressed professionally for her audition, she would go to the soundstage and dedicate herself to experiencing all a working film set had to offer.

A huge sign posted at the doorway stated that only authorized personnel were allowed.

"Miss, this is a closed set," said the security officer.

"I know. I think Kyle Weston put me on the list. I'm Catherine Leigh."

The guard gave her an odd look and scanned his list. "Yes, you have full clearance. Go through hair and makeup to make sure you're not interrupting anything."

"Okay, thanks."

A bit nervous, Cate walked through the labyrinth of equipment and closed areas until she found the makeup room. When she entered, two women—the stylist and makeup artist—sat in the chairs before the mirror, talking.

"Excuse me. I'm here to watch the filming," announced Cate.

The two women exchanged tense looks.

"Okay," said the older one in her mid-forties. "And who are you?"

"Oh, I'm Catherine Leigh."

"Are they expecting you?"

"I'm not sure. Kyle Weston put me on the list last week."

"You need to speak with the production assistant." Without hesitation, she called into her walkie-talkie. "Rachel, can you come to makeup, please?"

Awkwardly, Cate peered around the room, modeling a lopsided smile, trying not to make eye contact.

Rachel, the production assistant, entered quite harried. "What is it?" she asked shortly.

The women pointed at Cate.

"She's a guest of Kyle's," said the younger woman. "Full access. Can you show her where to watch the filming?"

Rachel looked at Cate. "Sure, follow me."

Calling back to the other ladies a swift, *nice to meet you*, Cate trailed behind the fast-paced PA.

"I'm Rachel, and you are?"

"Oh, sorry." She nearly tripped over some cables as she tried to keep up. "I'm Catherine Leigh."

"Yes, I remember your name from the list. Weren't you scheduled to be here last week?"

"Yes, but ..."

"It's fine. Big scene today, though. Wouldn't think you'd want ... Never mind ..." Rachel stared at her, shaking her head.

"Okay, this is vital," she cautioned. "When we get to the set, be totally quiet. They're about to start."

Leading Cate to the behind-the-camera side, Rachel moved a chair for her to sit in.

Although in a somewhat secluded area—too dark for her to be seen—Cate had a great view of the action.

"Don't move around too much on this chair. It can squeak," the PA whispered. "Just stay real still, okay?"

The set was the interior of an apartment. The director was in a huddle talking to Kyle and Bethany, his costar, the attractive woman on the cover of the tabloid. After a few minutes, they stepped behind the doorway wall out of sight, and the first assistant director began to call the actions.

Kyle and Bethany entered fervently kissing and stripping each other of their clothing. Shocked, Cate was immediately aware she was watching the making of a love scene and any minute now, she would see one or both of them practically naked. Now it made sense—all the strange looks she received! And, come to think of it, Kyle had explicitly said last week was the best time for her to come for a visit.

The proper thing would be to stealthily leave the soundstage and run back home, pretending none of this happened. However, there was no way to depart without causing a disturbance. No movements, Rachel had warned her. Even a slight move in her chair might cause a creak. Barely breathing, she had to remain still. And despite her horror, she was intrigued by the process. No, it was Kyle who she couldn't take her eyes off. She forgot that leaving would be the polite thing to do. His body was perfectly cut and manly.

The scene was intense; both actors now movie set naked. She knew this was too accurate. They had been dating according to the tabloid throughout the filming, and if she were a fly on the wall, this must be what it looked like when they were together. Cate couldn't handle it. She squeezed her eyes shut. Eventually, she heard the director call "cut." Relief filled her. At least it was over.

"Back to one." The command rang through her wits. Cate's mind silently screamed. *Not again!*

It started over. This time, it was even more passionate than the first take, lips touching the bare parts of their bodies. It was difficult to miss Bethany's attributes—a svelte and sexy woman.

Cate pictured her own body—slim and shapely, girlish, yet not quite matured to womanly.

Again, she forced her eyes shut, keeping them closed until she heard "cut and wrap for the night."

Silently rising from the chair, Cate tried to find her way out. *Oh, no!* Bethany and Kyle were walking straight toward the area right in front of her. She sank deeper into the shadows.

Dressed in their robes, Bethany reached out to Kyle's arm.

"Aren't you as horny as I am?" she laughed. "Maybe tonight we should do this for real."

Still in the shadows, having heard enough of their conversation, Cate crept unseen to the doorway and escaped.

Kyle stared at Bethany with a disapproving glint. "I thought you were engaged."

"What he doesn't know won't hurt him. And Kyle, you make me so hot," she cooed seductively. "We can meet at your place."

"Sorry, Bethany, I've an obligation tonight. And so do you ... to your fiancé."

He headed out of the soundstage to his dressing room trailer, leaving his costar indignantly miffed.

⚛

Cate had sidestepped Kyle's trailer and rushed around the corner as fast as she could, trying to find a route to the parking lot. Reeling to a stop, she was at a dead-end. She'd have to go back.

As she slinked by the trailer and started down the street, she heard, "Cate?!"

Slowly, she turned around to face Kyle, now dressed in jeans with no shirt, hanging out his door.

"Cate, what're you doing here?"

Hesitantly, she walked back to him. "I had an audition and thought I'd walk the lot a bit." She scoured the area. "I'm lost. Can't find the parking."

"This is great. Give me a minute to finish getting dressed, and I'll walk you. Hey, why don't we get some dinner?"

The words spurted from Cate's lips, "Oh, I thought you'd be busy tonight."

He wrinkled his brow. "No, why do you think that? Let me get a shirt on. Wait there."

His smile was so welcoming it astonished her.

As he closed the door, excitedly grabbing his shirt, his mind precipitously wandered … if only that love scene had been with Cate. He pushed down the thought.

Outside, Cate still plotted her flight. If only she could slip away right now.

As Kyle exited his trailer, his smile illuminating at her presence, Rachel walked out the soundstage door.

"Hey, Kyle. Call-time change for tomorrow," she said, handing him a fresh sheet and then turned to Cate. "So, did you enjoy the filming today, Ms. Leigh?"

"Ahhh … yes." Cate was shamefaced.

"See you in the morning, Kyle." Swiftly, Rachel rushed back through the door.

Staring at Cate, who was cringing, Kyle tried not to laugh. "You watched the love scene?"

She gulped. "I had no idea what you were shooting today. I didn't know until it was too late. I couldn't leave without disrupting everything," she rattled off. "So, I sat there with my eyes closed." It was partly true, she rationalized.

"You sat there through the whole filming with your eyes closed?"

"It'd be impolite to stare," she babbled, dropping her head.

He chuckled. "It's acting, Cate. That's not how it really is."

Cate watched him, searching for the right words. "She's your girlfriend."

"No, she's not. We just went to dinner one night after filming to discuss the script."

"Isn't she expecting you tonight?" She removed the tabloid from her purse and placed it into his hands, indicating the cover photo facing upward.

"How do you …?" He became aware of how wounded she seemed. "This is garbage, Cate. Really, there's nothing. She's engaged. That goes against my moral compass." Passing a trash bin, he threw the tabloid into it. "Cate, you're the one I wanna spend time with. You're my true friend."

At the parking lot, they approached her car. "Let's get a bite," he said, opening the car door for her. "Where would you like to go?"

Out of the blue, Cate felt angry and couldn't figure out why. Kyle had done nothing to hurt her. So, why did she want to get away from him? Or did she really want him to take her in his arms and kiss her as he had in that stupid love scene?

"Home," she declared. "Thanks anyway, but I'm going home." She climbed into her vehicle and rolled down the window. "And thanks for letting me watch you film. Sorry, I picked the worst day," she said prickly.

Without another word, she started her car and drove away, leaving him perplexed.

Chapter 17
Transition

Cate sat at the manicurist's station next to Julia.

"I can't believe my agent's retiring," Cate groaned. "You can't survive in this town without good representation. Talk about feeling alone in the world. What do I do now?"

"I have some contacts," said Julia as the manicurist placed her fingers in the solution to soak. "I'll help you look."

"Would you please?! I'd appreciate it so much," she said, watching her nails being filed.

Nudging her, Julia noted, "You should bring it up to Joseph and Kyle."

Looking up sharply, she shook her head. "No, not Kyle."

"Why?"

"Because everybody uses Kyle. It's sick," Cate said gravely.

Julia sneered, "It's not like he's not getting something in return … and you know what I mean." Tempering her cynicism, she conceded, "Okay, not Kyle. You could talk to Joseph. He's a pal."

Cate wrinkled her nose. "So is Kyle."

"Of course. But you're right. He gets used a lot because of who he is."

Exhaling weightily, Cate moaned, "If I can't find a new agent, maybe I should go home."

"Back to San Diego? You can't leave, Cate. What would I do

without you? You're my only real friend. I promise I'll use my connections to find you an agent."

∞

Joseph was lying on his sofa, reading over his script for next week's filming of the episode. On a break from his out-of-town production, Kyle gave Joseph a call.

"Hey, Kyle," Joseph answered. "How's the shoot?"

"It's good," began Kyle. "I'll be relieved when this guest star role wraps. TV's too fast-paced for my taste. I'm tired of being on the road."

"And I see you have a new distraction," kidded Joseph.

"She's exhausting. It won't last."

"When does it ever?"

"How's Cate?" Kyle asked quietly, a pang of guilt at the back of his mind.

"I'm a little worried about her."

"Why?"

"Her agent decided to close shop, so she's been interviewing other agencies." He set down his script. "She had a bizarre experience the other day."

"What happened?" Kyle felt an odd anxiousness.

"Listen to this. Cate had an appointment to interview this agent late one afternoon. She waited in the reception area with the secretary, who was about to quit for the day. The agent buzzed for her to come in, and the secretary left."

"They're alone?"

"Yeah, but let me get to the strange part. Cate enters to see the agent sitting in a bear costume behind his desk."

"A bear costume like for Halloween?" He laughed and then stopped himself. "I shouldn't laugh."

"I did until I realized Cate's too polite to turn and leave." Joseph rubbed his forehead. "The guy contended he always did this to test if actresses could keep in character when thrown a curve. It was a tool he used."

"That's terrible," scoffed Kyle, muting various cruder words he could have used.

"There's more. She picked up the script from his desk, took a seat, and read. Cate said she was concentrating hard on the script when she realized he had stepped out from behind the desk and was leaning on it in front of her. She looked up, and he had nothing on from the waist down … hanging it out maybe a couple feet from Cate's face."

"Holy shit!" Kyle sat up abruptly. "Dear God, tell me she ran out of there."

"Yes, they did a lap around his desk, and she tore out of the place. She called me after. She was pretty shaken up."

"Who is this guy?!" he said furiously. "That's disgusting. One of us should have been there."

"Kyle, we both know that's impossible, but she did ask me to go to the next interview with her. She's intimidated."

"You mean she's scared shitless?" Kyle paused, sympathetic. "I feel so bad for Cate. Finding representation is tough enough without this kind of crap."

"Anyway, I talked to my agent to see if she's accepting new clients, and she isn't."

"Damn. Neither's Tom," he groaned. "He may at least meet her as a favor to me."

"Thanks, Kyle. I hate for her to return to San Diego."

Kyle's voice rattled. "Is she contemplating that?"

"It's an option."

"I'll call Tom now." Kyle hung up.

Joseph smiled to himself as he picked up his script.

Julia answered her office phone, tracking the mess of expenses for the new series in pre-production.

"Hello."

"Julia, I can't believe you did it!" Cate was livid.

"Did what? Why're you angry?"

"You called Kyle and told him I was losing my agent, didn't you," she blasted.

"Oh, that. I did, but I wasn't the first to bring it up." Proceeding to add numbers, Julia asked, "Why? Didn't he help?"

"Of course he did! His management team signed me."

"Congratulations. You should be taking me to lunch, not bitching at me." Julia miscounted and had to start over.

"You know I didn't wanna take advantage of Kyle's friendship," she griped.

"Come on, Cate. Kyle was happy to do it. You're a friend, not one of those bimbos who figure he'll make them a star."

"Sounds pretty similar to me," Cate pronounced.

"No, it's not." She pounded on the clear key of the calculator. "Besides, if it makes you feel any better, he'd heard what happened from Joseph before I asked."

"Heard *what* from Joseph?!"

"That you were shopping for a new agent. Why?" She stopped and listened intently. "Is there more?"

"Sort of. I'll give you details later, but I interviewed with this creepy agent."

"Do I need a cocktail for this?"

"Oh, it's a nightmare!"

Julia pushed away her work.

"Anyway, Cate, Kyle talked to his agent after Joseph planted the seed! Everything's fine. C'mon. Let's celebrate and go crazy in your nice-girl way. We'll have a spa day ... mani-pedi, massage, facial! And you can tell me all about that creepy jerk."

Kyle flopped down on his couch to answer his phone as Pepper excitedly jumped onto his lap, licking his chin, tail wagging madly.

"Okay, Pepper," he laughed, "I'm on the phone."

"Kyle?" a voice on the other end said.

"Hey, Cate. Sorry, Pepper's going nuts. He's thrilled I'm home."

"Well, we've all missed you."

"Thanks. It's nice to be back, that's for sure."

Cate took a deep breath, steadying herself. "Kyle, thank you for recommending me to Tom."

"Of course."

"But, Kyle, I didn't want to use your influence. I mean, I so appreciate it, but that's not why we're friends."

"Cate, it's you. You're not like others. I wouldn't have done it if I didn't believe you were incredibly talented. And besides, if memory serves me, you didn't ask. Everyone else did," he chuckled.

"Yeah," she blushed even though no one could see. "I have good friends."

"We both do."

―※―

The four got together at Trent's establishment.

When Julia and Cate arrived, Joseph and Kyle were in a private deliberation. Seeing the ladies, the conversation immediately halted. They greeted each other. Julia ordered a rum and coke, and Cate, her usual, a ginger ale.

After kicking around the fellas' most recent jobs and Julia's headaches with production costs, the discussion turned to Cate and her new representatives.

"It's wonderful!" She was upbeat and sunny. "I've been to more auditions with Tom's firm in a month than six months with my old agent."

Joseph looked at Kyle and turned his attention to Cate. "Seen any bears lately," he joshed.

Kyle added with a snicker, "Was it Yogi, Smokey, or Winnie?"

The guys laughed. Cate was not amused. Neither was Julia.

"Ah, c'mon, it's a joke," Joseph dismissed.

"Cate, why didn't you leave the second you walked in?" asked Kyle.

Lowering her head, she placed her hands beneath her knees. "That would've been rude."

Joseph elbowed his cohort. "See, I told you."

Kyle nodded and then turned serious. "Cate, he didn't deserve courtesy, considering he had no pants on."

"I didn't know that at the time," she snapped.

Joseph almost laughed but didn't, a strained silence covering the table.

"Excuse me, I'm going to the ladies' room," Cate announced, hurrying away.

When she was out of sight, Julia railed at them.

"You guys are idiots. It's not funny. She could've been hurt," she admonished, rising from the table to follow Cate. "She's too trusting. And you're supposed to be her friends!"

Chapter 18
Little Girl Lost

A fabulous dancer and gifted teacher, Lisa Warrington instructed an afternoon dance class. In her late twenties with long, gleaming blonde hair and a flawless figure, she carried an air of sharp experience and maturity.

Cate felt fortunate that her instructor showed an interest in her talent. Several times, they met for coffee, discussing their hopes and dreams.

"G'afternoon, class," announced Lisa. "Today, a producer, Mr. Rex Talbert, will be observing. He's casting a musical feature and wants to see your dancing abilities. Consider this an initial audition."

While having been well-trained in ballroom dance, Cate felt on edge doing an impromptu choreographed routine. This wasn't how she was used to auditioning, and she wasn't convinced she'd want to be in a musical. The issue was singing. Although she was getting a little less self-conscious the more she sang with Kyle, she certainly had not overcome her fear.

The producer—a highly muscular man, six foot three, with mousy brown hair, in his late thirties, although he appeared more worn than that—took notes and solely spoke to Cate's instructor.

As Cate unlocked her apartment door, thirty minutes after the dance class audition, the phone rang.

"Hi Catherine, I have marvelous news," Lisa began readily. "Mr. Talbert said he only found one actor he's considering casting in the film, you. Grab your headshot and resume. Come out with us for coffee. Give me your address, and I'll pick you up in a few minutes."

"Lisa, I'm a mess, hot and sweaty from class. Besides, I think I need to run this by my agent. Could I, maybe, set up an audition tomorrow instead?"

"No!" She answered a bit too bluntly. "Don't be concerned about your agent. You'll be doing him a favor when you get the part, and he still rakes in the commission for it." She wrestled a chuckle. "This is your big break. It's only coffee. Freshen up, and I'll pick you up in twenty minutes. I insist!" And she hung up.

Holding the phone, Cate listened to the dial tone. Her gut told her not to go. She knew she should call back immediately and tell Lisa she felt sick—any excuse. And yet, being of two minds, another told her to be fearless when an opportunity presented itself. If she ever expected to do well in the business, she had to stop being timid. Besides, she'd be with Lisa.

The car rolled to a stop in front of Cate's building. Lisa lowered her window and shouted, "Let's get going. Stardom awaits!"

Cate reluctantly opened the passenger door.

They drove up to a free-standing office. "I thought you said coffee shop," Cate questioned.

"My mistake. They're in the middle of casting." Lisa prattled, "You'll meet important people here. You have your resume?"

Leaving the vehicle, Cate examined the area. Something seemed off. She had no idea where she was. She had never been to this part of North Hollywood, if they were even in North Hollywood anymore. The booming sound of a church's clock tower tolling the hour filled her fragile sentience.

They entered a one-room, nearly empty lease space, and no one was there except Talbert. A troubled nervousness overtook her.

"Lisa, thanks for coming, although you're late." The producer reached over and clicked off the CD. "Everyone's left. No problem. I have a few minutes. I'm happy to interview your friend." He stepped out from behind the conference table, covered with headshots and resumes, and lunged toward her, too ingratiating. "And you're the young lady from Lisa's class. Hello, Catherine. Rex Talbert. As mentioned earlier today, I'm producing *Songbird's Melody.*" He spied her motionless stance. "May I see your resume?"

Cate stiffly nodded.

He snatched the headshot from her. Inspecting the picture, he jeered and flipped it over to skim her resume.

"Oh, Lisa, before I forget, there's a package for you on the table."

He turned back to Cate. "Impressive. However, I don't see any singing or dance credits listed."

"Rex, Catherine hasn't had the opportunity yet, but you saw her in my class. She knows how to move." Lisa's voice sounded far away, having stepped back several feet behind Cate after retrieving the package.

"Yes, you do," he said, distinctly leering. "You'll need more experience, of course. I can help you with that."

All mixed up, voices clamored in Cate's head, and shrieked for her to run.

"I'm sorry, Mr. Talbert, please don't inconvenience yourself. I'll have my agent contact you, and we can set up another time when everyone's here." She called behind to her friend, "Lisa, I need to go." She heard what sounded to be a car door slamming. Suddenly, the noise of a car peeling away from the front of the building brought terror.

Rushing to the window, she spotted the car's taillights growing dimmer in the creeping darkness. The sun had set.

"Where's she going?!" Cate could hear herself yelling, a restrained panic in her voice.

"Lisa had another engagement. Don't worry. I'll drive you home ... after."

Cate rotated slowly to gawk at him. "After what?"

Staring at her, he turned on the CD player. She froze at the start of the song ... the boom of the bell chiming eerily imprisoning her awareness, each beat of her heart becoming more significant ... AC/DC's *Hell's Bells*.

An evil cackle emanated from Talbert as he raised the volume to a piercing level.

Darting full speed to the door, Cate yanked at the knob. Talbert seized her arm and threw her back into the office, bolting the door.

"Time to audition."

※

Wincing with each step, Cate entered her apartment, securely locking the door, her hands uncontrollably shaking. She hobbled to the bathroom.

Sitting in the corner of the shower floor, the hot water stung her bruised and cut skin while she numbly tried to unearth enough strength to take the next breath. She was in shock, constrained to crush the images in her mind, constantly reignited by the pain of the water on her raw wounds.

※

Her eyes fixed on the clock, her mind blank. She watched as each minute clicked by in the dead of the night. She became aware of how long sixty seconds was ... forever. She sat on the floor against the living room wall, staring at the locked door, a butcher knife beside her left leg. Grabbing it, almost unconsciously, she kept it close. Why, she had no idea. Perhaps it was her version of a security blanket. How impractical. Again, she lifted the knife with her trembling left hand. Her right wrist felt, at best, sprained, at worst, broken.

Just as her thoughts were emptied, giving an uncommon sense of calm, images would erratically flood her mind. Reality tarnished what could have been. He didn't take her to the desert to kill and shallowly bury her in the hot sand ... but he could be back ... any minute! She scrutinized her distorted, discolored wrist, seeing him drag her, twisting it forcefully to throw her against the table.

As if viewing through a slow-motion kinetoscope, she saw the headshots and resumes—symbols of her defiled ambition—scatter to the floor, printed images witnessing the abuse. As he violently pinned her upper arms, she screamed in agony. It was only the overture ... the symphony of suffering, a savage beating into submission, her sorrowful pleading intended to stop him seemed to instead provoke the meting out of even more ruthless pain ... cresting at the tearing away of clothes and his forcing himself inside her ... horrendously ripping her soul from her body. Watching from above like a ghost hovering over a dying child, the reality of destruction infected her consciousness.

How did she get home? It was a blur ... ducking his relentless punches into her distended abdomen.

Pointing the knife at the door when she heard footsteps on the walkway outside becoming louder, her heart pounded furiously. Heading perhaps to her door and then drifting further away—the key in the lock next door assured her this was her neighbor—the police officer—after his night shift. Cate, relieved, respired her fright, setting down the knife, tears streaming down her face as she again studied the clock tick away each minute until daylight.

⚜

Early the following morning, Cate made it to the free clinic in almost a trance, not recalling the drive there. Nearly all the clinic personnel she had to speak with were male. Maybe it was divine intervention. They were all considerate and careful in addressing her terror-infested emotions. The in-take clinic attendant inquired if she wouldn't prefer to go to the rape crisis center. Cate feared telling the authorities—she knew how it would go. Her life would be violated even more.

They repeatedly requested to contact a family member or a friend. She wanted no one to know. Everyone would see her differently—lacking, flawed, ruined. Every part of what she knew as her was gone.

After the examination and treatment, a psychiatrist who volunteered at the clinic sat with Cate and the medical doctor. Both, again, tried to convince her to obtain solace in the arms of her family and friends.

"No, he won't win. He won't make me run," she mumbled in response.

"Sometimes," the doctor advised, "you just have to walk away."

⚜

That evening, Cate hauled herself to acting class. She sat in the corner of the furthest row of chairs, away from everyone.

When it was her turn to read the sides, she begged to be an observer, refusing to abandon her seat. Edna roundly reminded her she was there to practice her craft, but Cate merely stared off in a haze.

At the end of the class, Edna asked Joseph if he knew why Cate was so withdrawn.

He shrugged. "I don't know."

"Mr. Beason, you're her friend. Go find out."

Joseph spotted Cate, with her purse ineptly held, reach to open the door. Seeing him coming towards her, she quickly exited the building.

As he ran to catch up with her, he hollered, "Cate, wait! Hey, what's going on?"

"Nothing, I have to go."

He saw her right wrist was wrapped in a brace, forcing her to hold her hand strangely. Gasping in pain with each breath, she pressed her arms tightly over her stomach. There was dark bruising on her upper arms. Joseph turned her chin to notice she was camouflaging with makeup a large bruise on the left side of her face.

"Oh my God, Cate, what happened?"

"I ..." Her mind was befuddled, plundered. "I was in a car accident."

He glanced around the parking lot. "Isn't that your car? It's fine."

"I was a passenger. I was riding with my dance teacher. If I'm a mess, she's worse." The lies were flowing.

"Are you hurt? You seem to be having trouble breathing."

"Yeah, cracked rib. I have a bad headache. I might've hit my head." Not true. She truly hoped it would end the interrogation.

"Cate, you could have a concussion." He took her left hand, and she slid it from his grasp.

"No, I'm fine. I went to the doctor."

Wanting to run away and hide, she prayed to be alone.

"Did you tell your brother or your mom?" Joseph again reached out to touch her arm, to comfort her.

"No!" she curtly shouted. "No reason to tell them. I need some rest. Good night, Joseph."

She hurried to her car and drove away.

The following weeks, she missed class, and Joseph's efforts to check on her went straight to her answering machine. He was exasperated. He had to concentrate on a TV detective drama. It was one of his most significant breaks, and he wanted to share the news with Cate, who was suddenly unreachable.

Kyle had been on location in Seattle for the past month. After hearing about Joseph landing the recurring role in the series, he immediately phoned.

"I'm happy for you. When's your first episode?"

"Next week."

"That's incredible. Edna'll be putting another notch in her coaching belt. She's probably bursting with pride," asserted Kyle.

"Yeah, how's your shoot going?" Joseph slyly commented, "I noticed your costar, huh? Jeniene, she's hot."

"It's fun."

"You gonna be home for the holidays?" he asked.

"Should be wrapped by Christmas. I plan to spend the four-day Thanksgiving break here with Jeniene."

"Maybe come across some time to focus on your script?" Joseph advised.

"Right," Kyle faltered, pushing forward. "How's Cate? I keep calling. I only get her machine."

"I don't know. I haven't seen or talked to her in weeks."

"What do you mean?" Kyle's concern could be heard in his elevated tone. "Hasn't she been to Edna's?"

"Not for two weeks. Edna's not happy either. She specifically told me she has a long waiting list of potential students and hates to do it, but if Cate doesn't show up to the next class, or at least call with an excuse, she's giving her spot away."

"That doesn't sound like Cate. She doesn't blow off classes."

"I guess the car accident was worse than she thought."

"What accident?!" Kyle's tone was urgent.
"About three weeks ago, she was pretty banged up."
Silence …
Kyle battled heightened anxiety.

Chapter 19
Solitude

The rays of light streaming through the darkening curtains created distorted shapes on the ceiling. Since the rape, Cate had barely slept, tossing and turning at the fear endlessly plaguing her mind. She grew weary of the haunting.

She had to get out of the darkest abyss of her life. Coaching her shattered mind … *it's time to be courageous, defiant, attack life with tenacity. I have formidable, untapped power. Nothing will deter me. I need to be me again.*

Her passion energized her—and then, she arrived at her mom's for Thanksgiving dinner.

The family home was scented with turkey and freshly baked apple pie. Family photos lined the fireplace mantel. Cate stared at a picture of her father holding her in his arms on her third birthday. They both were full of joy. Her melancholy grew; her dad dead for three years now. How she missed him. He'd make everything better. The irony was even if she could sit with him, talk to him, hug him, she'd never tell him about that night. This was her burden to bear … alone.

"Catherine, you're not eating. Please eat, dear." Doris passed the stuffing to her son. "And, darling, why do you have your jacket on?"

Staring at her plate of food, Cate resigned not to look up. "I'm a little cold."

"What's wrong with you today?" Edward asked, passing the stuffing to Cate. "You're usually fighting with me over the turkey legs."

She set the plate in the center of the table, taking no portion for herself.

"I don't feel well. I might be coming down with something." She hung her head, refolding the napkin beside her empty plate.

Doris placed the broccoli casserole in front of Cate. "Oh, sweetheart. I hate it when you don't feel well. I'll make you a large plate to have when you're better."

"Sure, Mom, thanks." With her palm over her forehead, she grimaced. "I'm sorry, I need to go."

She rose from the table and went into the living room. Doris followed her daughter and placed her hand gently against her cheek to feel whether she was warm. Then she bent forward and put her upper lip on Cate's forehead—an Italian mother's way to check for a temperature.

"You're not feverish, Catherine. All the same, why don't you lie down for a bit in your room? It's early, not even noon. Take a little nap."

Edward came into the room and studied his sister. He knew, even sick, this was not her normal behavior.

"Yeah, be happy you have your room. Mom made mine her dance studio."

"Thanks, Mom, but I'd rather rest at my apartment." Her vision glued on her father's picture again.

"Honey, it's Thanksgiving weekend. I want you to stay."

Before Cate could respond, the phone rang. "Let me get this ..." Doris said as she quickly headed to the kitchen.

"Mary! ... Hey, kids," she hollered back to them, "it's your Aunt Mary."

"Happy Thanksgiving, Aunt Mary," yelled Edward.

As their mother became trapped in conversation with her sister, Edward continued to study Cate.

"What's going on with you? You've been staring at Dad's picture all morning."

"I told you, I'm sick. Tell Mom I love her, and I had to go." She strode to the mantel, snatched the photo of her father, and put it in her jacket pocket. "I'm making a copy of this."

Her brother blocked the door. "Catherine, are you okay?"

"I'm fine. I need to go. Happy Thanksgiving." She gave him a perfunctory hug and rushed out the door.

With a ragged breath, her hands on the steering wheel, she slowly turned the ignition, fighting the tears to drive the long trek home.

Climbing the stairs, Cate dragged herself to her apartment. At least here at home, she would be allowed her misery. Coming closer to her apartment door, she was shocked to see Kyle sitting on the stoop.

"Kyle, what're you doing here?"

"Excuse me, that's a lousy hello." He stood, brushing off the dust. "I flew from Seattle to wish you a Happy Thanksgiving."

Gradually, her warmth crept out. "Thank you. How long have you been waiting?"

"I came straight from the airport here. Since you never seem to answer your phone anymore, I took a chance I might catch you before you went to your mom's. I was giving it a few more minutes. So glad you came home." He noticed her jittery demeanor. "May I come in?"

She hesitated. "Sure."

Cate's place, which always felt welcoming with her energy, had an air of darkness and dread, even though Kyle could not perceive what might have changed. The furniture was the same. It was neat and clean. Maybe too clean. He could smell disinfectants and bleach instead of her perfume.

"You flew from Seattle to visit me?" She set down her jacket on the sofa, taking the photo from the pocket and placing it next to the ones of her mom and brother.

"Yes, you and my grandmother." He gestured to the photo. "Who's that?"

"It's my dad and me at my birthday party."

Picking up the picture, he smiled joyfully. "You were a beautiful child. I bet he was a great dad."

"He was. I loved him so much. I was happy. Holidays always make me miss him more." Cate shook the mental fog away. "Would you like something to drink?"

"Just water," he said, setting the photo next to the others.

She opened her compact refrigerator to get the pitcher.

Coming up behind her to get his drink, Kyle brushed against her shoulder. Cate jumped and screamed.

He backed away, shocked. "Cate, I didn't mean to startle you."

"I'm sorry." Her heart pounding violently, she combated her emotions.

"Cate, you don't have to be sorry. Is this the car accident?"

She saw him staring at the bruises on her upper arms and hastily covered them with her hands, pulling down on the short sleeves of her blouse to lengthen them, her thick bracelet on her right wrist sliding down to allow discoloration to be seen.

"Who told you that?" She appeared frightened.

"Joseph."

She couldn't lie to Kyle. "It wasn't ..." Repressing her words, she also couldn't tell him the truth.

"It wasn't what?" he asked.

She shook off his quiz with a meek guise.

"Joseph also told me you won't call him back," Kyle continued. "Why? And Edna's getting upset. If you miss another class, she may replace you."

"Thank you for telling me. I won't miss another."

Focusing on her sad eyes, he sympathized. "Not doing well?"

She suddenly had an overwhelming urge to hug ... and tell him everything.

"I'm fine," she murmured.

He tenderly cupped her face in his hands. "Okay, get your jacket then."

"Why?"

"We're visiting my grandmother." He marched over and picked up her jacket, holding it out to her.

"No, Kyle, I'm not up to it." Cate slowly sat on her sofa, defeated.

"C'mon." He puckered his face and tugged on her hand. "You must get out of this absurdly disinfected apartment."

⁂

Traveling toward Costa Mesa, Kyle turned on the radio. "Wanna play our music game?"

Cate smiled reticently, reaching for the radio knob, and shut it off. "Sorry, headache."

"No problem."

After a moment of silence, it occurred to Cate that Kyle had flown hundreds of miles spontaneously to be with her. She looked at him lovingly. "Thank you."

"For what?"

"For being here."

He kissed her hand and held it for the rest of the trip to his grandmother's.

⁂

It was evening when they entered Nana's home for a Thanksgiving feast. She greeted them with hugs, Pepper at her feet, wagging his tail.

Regarding Cate, Nana knew something was awry. They ate turkey, and Kyle spoke spiritedly about his shoot. Even though the conversation was light, Nana never stopped concentrating on her. As the dinner wound down, Cate began to clear the table and stack the dishwasher in the kitchen.

Shifting over, Nana crunched a ten-dollar bill in her grandson's hand.

"What's this for?" he laughed.

"Please run to the grocery store and buy some whipped cream for the pumpkin pie."

"We don't need whipped cream."

"We do," she said, patting his hand. "Go get it, please, sweet boy."

"Cate?" he shouted to invite her to go with him.

"No," Nana corrected, "You go and get it."

Wiping her hands with a dish towel, Cate entered the dining room and asked, "Did you call me?"

Nana held Kyle's attention. He took the hint.

"I'm being sent to the store to get some whipped cream. Keep Nana and Pepper company?"

"Of course," agreed Cate with a big smile.

Starting for the door, Kyle looked back when he heard his grandmother say to Cate, "Come here, dear, sit with me." Pepper hopped onto Cate's lap, nosing her hand to pet him.

∞

It was nearly impossible to locate a store open on Thanksgiving. Kyle was gone for almost an hour before discovering a mini-market open. Luckily, it had whipped cream.

Gavrhel

Barreling into the house, bushed from his scavenger hunt, he bellowed, "Nana, that pie had better be worth this effort."

He intruded upon a confidential scene. Nana was holding Cate, collapsed in sobs, rocking her tenderly in her arms, comforting her. "Everything'll be fine, I promise, sweet girl."

His grandmother met his eye and motioned for him to leave them alone. Taking off his jacket, he left the room and sat outside on the porch swing, Pepper jumping onto his lap.

Kyle opened the paper bag, took out the whipped cream, shook the can, and squirted some into his own mouth. Pepper wagged his tail eagerly, staring up at Kyle's face.

"What? You want some?" Kyle put a little whipped cream on his finger, and glanced nervously over his shoulder. "Okay, but just a little, and don't let Nana know."

A half-hour later, Nana came out to him.

"What's going on? Is she all right?" Kyle was deeply concerned.

"She will be." Nana affectionately squeezed his arm. "How much do you know?"

"Nothing. Tell me what's wrong, Nana, please."

"Cate'll tell you when she's ready. Give her time."

Scouring his feelings, he acquiesced. "Okay."

Reassuring, she sat beside him. "It's not an easy conversation. She does need to talk. But she doesn't want to be judged."

"Why would I ever judge her?" He looked up, concentrating on the issue.

"You wouldn't." Nana paused and looked admiringly at her grandson. "Kyle, she trusts you. You've been a good friend to her. You need to be prepared to listen and not react."

"I'm an actor. I can do that." He gave a half-hearted laugh.

"You're also her friend. The reality may be difficult." She took his hand. "I'm so proud of you, sweet boy."

They sat silently for a time, Kyle attempting to discern Nana's meaning.

Finally, he held out the paper bag. "Here's what's left of the whipped cream. I was bored, so I had some."

"That's fine. I don't have anything to put it on anyway."

"What about the pie?"

"What pie? I don't have a pie." She smiled. "Why don't you two stop and buy a dessert on your way home."

Cate sullenly came out of the house.

"Thank you for coming for Thanksgiving, sweet boy," Nana said, handing him his jacket. "Remember, I love you."

He was taken aback. "We're leaving?"

"Yes, it's getting late," confirmed his grandmother as she caressed Cate's head with devoted tenderness. "You take care, sweet girl. Call me if you need anything or just want to talk."

Cate managed a cheerless smile. "Thank you." And she climbed into the car.

Nana hugged Kyle and pointed her finger in his face. "Remember, be a friend."

"Okay, Nana." He hiked to the car.

"Thank you for coming. I love you." She waved, Pepper barking his goodbye.

∞

The stillness in the car had been deafening during the long journey to Cate's apartment. Kyle finally turned on the radio. He glanced at her. Staring out to the night, her face reflected in the darkened window's sheen, a struggle against the morose.

Lost in her thoughts, Cate mourned her stolen innocence, aching to turn back time. Now, she could only dream how wonderful it would have been that the first man who touched her was someone she deeply loved and wanted. Not the nightmare of evil, terror, and pain.

Kyle could stand the silence no longer.

"Cate, I'm here, honey." Reaching over, he touched her cheek to bring her awareness of him.

Doing her utmost to hide her hopelessness, she dragged her sight to meet his gaze.

"I know," she said quietly and quickly looked down.

"Cate, please talk to me. Is this the accident? Please tell me the truth."

"I've never lied to you."

"Of course, I know."

Grimly, she pressed, "Then don't ask me to lie now."

"Catie, please."

She turned again to stare out the window.

When they neared their destination, the radio played Def Leppard's *Too Late for Love*. Kyle suddenly felt like a coward. He knew what he was now thinking. He didn't want the truth.

∞

Once they entered Cate's apartment, Kyle discovered where the disinfectant smell originated. In the bathroom sink was a white blouse soaking in a potent mixture of bleach and hot water.

"Cate, what's happening here?"

She looked over his shoulder. "Oh, it's my favorite blouse. I found it at the bottom of my laundry this morning. It had blood on the front. I was wearing it the day … I guess from …" She pulled the plunger to drain the sink, rinsed it, and wrung it out to hang over her shower curtain to drip dry, noticeably missing several buttons. "I was trying to salvage it."

"Why don't you buy another one?"

"It's the principle," she said sternly.

"Principle?"

She made light of it. "Not all of us are rich movie stars."

"I'll buy you a blouse," he graciously offered.

"You're not buying me clothes." She made a face. "It'd be weird."

They strolled to the living room, taking a seat on the sofa. There was a strain between them.

Grappling to find an opening, she asked, "When do you return?"

"Maybe tomorrow. I have a few days, although I should get back."

Again, silence uncomfortably cooled the room as she groped to bring up the subject.

"You were on the cover of a tabloid. She's pretty."

"Who?"

"Your costar." Her gaze transfixed him. "You happy, Kyle?"

"Sure." He was unconvincing, uneasiness overtaking him. "I'm gonna go. I'll talk to you in the morning. We can hang out before I make my flight." Picking up his jacket, he rose and started for the door.

She panicked. "Kyle, would you please stay with me?"

"What?" His mind began to race. Any other girl, he'd know what she meant. With Cate, he had no clue.

"I don't wanna be alone tonight," she pleaded.

"Are you asking me to spend the night?" He had to figure out what she expected.

"Please. It scares …" She muzzled her fears, avoiding saying too much. "I need a friend. And you're my very best."

"I am?"

"Yeah, you've always been. I trust you more than anyone."

Her words struck him. He realized it was good for him to live up to Cate's expectations, his grandmother's admonishment to *be a friend* echoing in his mind. Somehow, it allayed his tensions.

He relaxed.

At first, Kyle wondered where they'd be sleeping, and then he glimpsed Cate sitting on the sofa. He grasped the throw blanket, dragged up the ottoman to stretch out their legs, and sat beside her, holding her close. Tossing the blanket over them, Kyle turned off the sofa lamp, darkening the room.

Cate snuggled close, laying her head on his chest, and felt secure enough to sleep for the first time in weeks.

In the morning light, Kyle woke first. Still pressed against him, Cate was slightly angled away and sound asleep. The throw had slipped down and was covering their legs. The bottom of her blouse had crept up, exposing her slim abdomen. Darkness caught his eye. He peered down at her stomach, which was severely bruised. Even deeper and more pronounced than the bruises on her arms.

It was how he imagined a prize fighter's stomach would resemble after a vicious beating. He carefully lifted Cate's blouse to make out how far it spread. It went to her bra line, and he suspected higher. He could tell it probably went below her beltline as well. He gently replaced the blouse downward to cover her swollen skin. No way a car accident could do the level of damage inflicted short of putting her in the hospital. The bruises on her arms looked like someone had roughly grabbed her. They were at the same level on each arm and handprint-like. No longer wearing a bracelet, her wrist was terribly discolored, as if someone had gripped and twisted it.

Kyle roughly rubbed his head, trying to drive the evidence from his mind. How could this have happened? Beautiful, angelic Cate.

He lovingly combed his fingers through her hair.

Cate shifted her position on the sofa, turning away from him. Kyle slid deftly from her, stood up, grabbed his jacket, and quietly went to the door.

"Are you leaving?" she said groggily, rubbing her eyes and forcing herself to wake up.

"Yeah, I'm going home to shower and change. I'll be back in a couple of hours."

"Oh." She straightened the throw over her and tried not to show her disappointment.

"I need to make my flight reservation. I think I'll leave tomorrow instead." He began to open the door and stopped, looking back at her. She appeared so fragile.

An overwhelming need swelled in him. His brain worked overtime to sort out the dilemma.

"Cate, why don't you come back to Seattle with me?"

"Huh?" She was dazed.

"I'll get you a room. You can stay on location with me for the rest of the shoot. It might be fun to be a part of it."

"How would I be a part of it?" She stared at him, perplexed.

"Watching you work?"

"Sure, why not?" He started to walk back to her, having crafted a logical reason. "The more exposure to the workings of a movie set, the more comfortable you'll be when you finally get a chance to be in a film."

The concept was inviting, yet she drove it from her hopes.

"What would your costar think?" she asked tentatively.

His brow furrowed. "Her opinion's not important."

"I can't." She glanced up, heartbroken. Because? Her mind sought to locate a pretext. "I …"

"You what?" Stooping down before her, he held her hands.

Writhing, she stumbled upon an excuse. "I have Edna's class. You told me Edna would kick me out if I missed anymore."

"She'd understand. I'll call and tell her you're working with me in Seattle. She'd be thrilled and wouldn't mind you not being at class if you're in a project." He felt bound to convince her to come to the set to ensure she was with him. "I'll get a ticket, and you can fly back with me."

"Why do you want me there? Julia once told me you don't bring your girlfriends to your locations. They interfere with the serious business of acting. You're there to work, right?"

"This is different. We're *best* friends, remember?"

Kyle remained quiet about his need to protect her.

Although she yearned to go, she knew she couldn't. If her mom and brother had a problem with her attending a premiere with him, they would be beside themselves if they discovered she accompanied him to Seattle, no matter how harmless.

"I'd be in the way. And besides, it would look bad. The tabloids'll be all over the story."

"I don't care what those rags report." He stood up defiantly.

Holding the throw to her mouth as if to smother her true feelings, she sighed. "Let me think about it."

He pulled the blanket away from her face to look deeply into her eyes. "Please come with me," he implored.

She couldn't respond.

As he turned to go, he gazed at her affectionately. "I'll be back soon."

"Kyle?" She stopped him. "Thank you."

He knew the profoundly appreciative *thank you* was a *no*. He could hear it in her voice.

Chapter 20
My Sister's Keeper

"Catherine, what's going on?" Edward paced in front of her while she sat on her sofa, her hands under her knees, head hung low.

"Ever since the fall, you've been peculiar. First, Thanksgiving, and then saying you couldn't join us for Christmas because you had an audition. Bullshit! Since when does anyone work on Christmas? Catherine, you know how important holidays are to Mom." He noticed the photo of Cate and their dad and held it up. "By the way, when I talked to Mom last week, she mentioned this picture. I thought you were making a copy and giving it back."

"I am," she mumbled.

"You never answer your phone, forcing us to talk to your machine. You don't call back."

"Sorry, you didn't need to come over." Holding her hand in front of her mouth, she was reserved, despondent.

"I had to barge in to see if you're still alive!"

Frustrated, he stomped to her kitchen, opening the refrigerator to get a drink. Emptied of its contents, it was not running. "Catherine, what's going on with the refrigerator?"

"It's broken. I told the manager. He said he'd replace it soon."

Shaking his head, he stared at her skeptically. "How long's it been out of commission?"

She shrugged.

"So that's why you look so thin. You're not eating, are you?" He slammed the refrigerator door shut and walked back to where she sat.

"I'm okay," she said flippantly. "The camera puts ten pounds on you anyway."

"Catherine, I think you need to stay with me until he gets you a new one." Edward felt exasperated. He hadn't talked to her like this since they were kids ... but she deserved it.

"Nooo, not with Valerie there all the time. Thanks anyway." She sunk lower on her sofa, head back.

He yielded. "Fine. I'll call the manager."

After a long silence, his comportment softened. "I know you, Sis. You can't fool me. You've been different for two, three months." He gazed at her kindly. "I understand if you don't want Mom to know what's going on. I promise I won't tell her."

Cate rallied her acting skills. "Ed, please stop making something out of nothing. School's stressing me out. And I've been busy auditioning. If anyone should appreciate the pressure I'm under, it's you. You're sitting for the Bar in July."

Edward moved to the ottoman in front of Cate and held her hands. "Sis, did some guy break your heart?"

She gave a token laugh. "Whatever you're imagining's so wrong. I don't even have time to date. Not what you're thinking."

"You don't know what I'm thinking," he smirked.

But she did. In her mind, Edward assumed it was some guy, possibly Kyle, who shattered her spirits. And she was right.

Edward exploded.

"Did Kyle do something?"

"No, Edward. It wasn't some date, and it certainly wasn't Kyle. He'd never hurt me. I know that for a fact."

"Really?"

"Stop. It's not that. I told you I'm overworked, and it's getting to me."

If only it were that uncomplicated.

Ferreting out her withdrawn manner, he recognized his sister was living by the family creed: You got yourself into the mess, you get yourself out of it.

"Catherine, if you ever have a problem, you can come to me."

"Even married to Valerie?" She picked at the weave in her sofa's fabric, feeling sad she was losing the one person her whole life on whom she could rely.

"Of course, you're my sister. Nothing'll ever change that. I'm supposed to watch out for you. I swear I always will."

She nodded glumly.

"I think," he began, "we both need a concert to cheer us up. We haven't been to one since last summer. I'll check to see if the firm has tickets to a fun show."

"That's wonderful, thanks. But can you afford to take a night off from studying? The Bar's important."

"Yeah, we both could use a break," he said, hugging her. "Oh, but let's limit the amount of slugging band members. I only do so much legal work for free, even for family," he laughed.

Blushing, she chuckled, "I can still see Digger doubled over from my punch. What a jerk."

"Right to the gut," he joked. "I'm so proud of my little sister."

Edward always knew how to make her smile, and it reminded her that he was the best brother. The Leigh kids together were a dynamic pair.

Chapter 21
Friends and Lovers

It was the beginning of February, and the days could not have been more tranquil, announcing the arrival of an early Spring. The gang had finally been able to schedule an evening out together. The purpose was to introduce the group to Julia's new love, the man of her dreams.

Despite Kyle's busy schedule, he was far more available than Cate, who had avoided her pals since before Thanksgiving.

They met at their usual hang-out, Cate being the last to arrive. Kyle saw her first, noticing she carried a dejected posture. Once she came within sight of everyone else, her carriage immediately changed to welcoming and bright, scampering over to greet everyone. He took note of the transformation.

Julia's new beau, John Mantle, was a CPA who had just opened a firm in Los Angeles, garnering clients from the entertainment industry. He was tall, in his mid-thirties, and quite handsome.

Cate was sincerely happy for her friend and was almost peaceful, watching them gaze at each other dreamily. Nevertheless, Kyle continued to study Cate's chameleon moods. It only deepened his concern. The group discussed their careers and goals while taking turns on the dance floor.

Mid-evening, as the ladies excused themselves to find the powder room, Joseph went to talk with Trent, who ran the bar, leaving Kyle and John alone at the table, sitting in extended silence, both seemingly uneasy.

John finally managed the nerve to speak. "Julia tells me that the two of you used to date."

Still consumed by his anxieties over Cate, Kyle was startled. "We dated in high school. But that was long ago. We're friends now."

"Julia says that as well," said John. "You're merely friends."

Kyle recognized the distinct look on John's face—a man in love yet fearful of losing that love to someone else.

"John, I respect Julia and value her friendship. But I don't have any room in my life for a relationship."

"What about comfort?" John's face was shadowed with disquiet.

"No, nothing's going on," he pledged. "I'll always care for Julia as a pal. That's all."

Fiddling with the drink coaster, John was apprehensive. He sighed fitfully. "I love her very much, Kyle. She's the woman I've been searching for all my life." John paused. "I want her to be happy. I guess I need to ensure she's truly available."

"Believe me, she is."

"Of course I am, darling," said Julia as she walked up to the table with Cate. "Kyle had his chance, and in typical Weston fashion, he blew it." Friskily, she gave John a quick kiss. "Thank you for that, Kyle, or I might not have met this incredible man."

"Oh, that's so sweet," teased Joseph as he walked up, overhearing the table talk. "Kyle's short attention span benefits someone other than himself."

"Okay, okay," griped Kyle. "Hilarious."

"I think what Kyle's trying to say, John, is how happy he is for you and Julia," asserted Cate.

"Exactly. Thank you, Cate." He smiled warmly at her, then looked back to John. "I did need to meet with you, John, about business, though. I'm unhappy with my current accountant, and I'd like to discuss changing to your firm."

"Certainly." John was relieved. "We could meet for lunch on Monday."

"Sounds great," he said. "My treat."

"Maybe not after I take a look at your finances," jested John.

They all laughed in response as Julia cuddled her new love's arm.

Another round of drinks and dancing enlivened the party. Kyle, however, returned his concentration to Cate, who would shift from being engaged with the group to withdrawing inward. He still couldn't come to grips with what he knew deep down might have happened to her.

"Cate, you never really told me how you did last week at your audition for the comedy series." He moved closer to force her focus. "How was it?"

"It was okay," she answered quickly, turning away as she watched Julia and John return to the table after dancing. "John, how 'bout I show you some easy steps?"

"Oh yes, darling, please," Julia entreated. "Cate's an amazing dancer."

"And a good teacher," Joseph added.

"Okay, I'm game. Shall we, Cate?" John reached for Cate's arm, and they strolled out to the dance floor.

Leaning in, Kyle asked, "Have you two noticed Cate seems *off* tonight?"

"Off?" asked Joseph.

"Reserved, distant?" He became more earnest. "All evening, she's gravitated between participating, having fun, and being lost in her own world."

Julia and Joseph looked at each other, shrugging.

"Kyle, she's super busy with school trying to graduate in May," said Julia. "She's probably just preoccupied."

"Julia's right, Kyle. Cate's obsessed with studying," offered Joseph. "And yet when I see her at Edna's class, she's as enthusiastic as ever … her normal self."

"Okay," Kyle granted, "I haven't seen her since Thanksgiving when she was jumpy and scared, but I do talk to her on the phone, and lately, although she seems to be much happier landing so many roles these past months, there's still something going on. I can feel it. And the other day, she was unusually tense after that comedy interview."

Julia became agitated. "Did you ask her what happened?"

"Yeah, but she wouldn't say. And I don't think it was the interview. I believe it reminded her of something. That's why I asked about it. Didn't you see how she avoided the subject?"

"No, she answered your question," inserted Joseph. "Kyle, I don't see what's got you all worked up."

Kyle faced Julia. "Certainly, you've noticed Cate's been withdrawn."

"Like I said, she's exhausted."

"Maybe, Julia," appealed Kyle, "you could talk to her?"

Nibbling on the pretzels, she shook her head. "No, you should. She tells me all the time that you're her best friend."

"Yeah, she says that to me too, Kyle," grumbled Joseph. "Which has been annoying since I met her first."

Kyle wasn't listening, staring into his glass.

"I can't!" he blurted.

"Why?" Julia placed her arm on his shoulder. "If she tells anybody anything, it'd be you. Let her know it's safe to talk."

"If you don't do it, I will," Joseph asserted.

"No, Kyle needs to be the one," she advised. "He's the one who's noticed, not us." She touched Kyle's arm. "Be brave, *Mister Movie Star*. After all, she's a girl. You do well with the female sex."

"A girl who's your friend!" reminded Joseph.

John and Cate returned to the table, a bit winded.

"Gee, you two looked great!" Joseph proclaimed.

"Honey, Cate may make you a dancer yet." Julia gave John another loving kiss.

Rising to go to the restroom, Kyle looked back at Cate and watched her smile melt into discomfort as the attention was shifted from her to John. Only Kyle saw, reigniting his worry.

Chapter 22
Kyle's Best Friend

Cate opened her door at the knock, Kyle leaning against the door frame.

"Well, Mister Weston, this is a pleasant surprise," she beamed. "What brings you to this neck of the woods on this fine afternoon?"

"Can we talk?" he said quietly.

"Sure. You sound serious. Am I in trouble?"

"Absolutely not." He entered and immediately went to her kitchen, opening the refrigerator to browse its contents.

She frowned at his brashness. "Looking for something?"

"Yeah, I'm looking for a drink." Kyle bent forward, moving the fruit juice cartons aside.

"There's water and juice," she offered.

He popped his head around the corner. "Something with a little more of a kick."

"Still underage," she said, putting her hands out.

Pouring a glass of water, he crossed to the sofa and patted the seat next to him. "Come sit."

His dire nature was disturbing. She felt she was about to be scolded and didn't know why.

Gathering he was ill-prepared for what would occur, Kyle endeavored to begin the painful dialogue.

"Cate." He took her hand. "You're so wonderful, and I accept you always."

"O … kay," she tentatively answered.

"You can trust me, Cate. I'm on your side."

She stared at him.

"I believe I know you better than most people," he continued. "You're the best person I've ever met. And you're innocent."

When the word *innocent* fell from his lips, she realized what he aimed to discuss, causing her mind to flash alarm.

"Talk to me, please. I'll listen, and I won't run away."

Cate tried to speak, aware other than with Nana, she had never verbalized the event, even to herself. As she attempted to form the words, the memory she had diligently tried to bury into the lower recesses of her subconscious came cascading to the forefront of her mind. It was overwhelming. She pushed away from him to press herself tightly into the corner of the sofa, as far from him as she could get. Her feet on the sofa seat, she towed her legs up to her chest to make herself small and self-contained.

This was not the response he hoped to see—she was petrified.

Steadying himself, he breathed out. "If you can't, I'll say it." He hoped the words he next used would make her appreciate that he had accepted her. "Last fall, it wasn't a car accident. You were horribly beaten."

Her chin quivered, tears pooling. He sipped his water, stalling. With a heavy sigh, he persevered.

"The bruises. You were covered in bruises, and it was three weeks after. I can't even imagine how violent it was."

Trying to compose himself, he studied her. "Cate, please tell me. Were you raped?"

Cate burst into tears, unable to speak.

Kyle's mind rebelled. His grandmother was right. He wasn't ready for his suspicions to be confirmed, but he had to be strong for Cate. Folding her into his arms, he held her gently and whispered, "Catie, I'm here for you."

"I …" she wavered, resting her head against his chest.

"Catie, take your time … but please tell me now."

Uselessly wiping the moisture from drenching her cheeks, a heaviness suffocating her, she peeked at him. "I was stupid. I trusted the wrong person. I believed she was a friend."

"*She*?"

Steeling herself, Cate forced the truth out. "My dance teacher. She pressured me into going. And even drove me to where there was supposed to be an audition. There wasn't. He wasn't really … it wasn't real. And when I turned around, she was gone. She just left me there with him. I guess they were a team. I tried to confront her a few days later, and the dance studio said she moved away unexpectedly."

"I understand." He could feel her silence closing in, her terror now resurrected.

"How did you get home?" he began again. "Wait, you don't have to tell me."

"After …" She choked on her breath, "he threw me in his car. I had no idea where we were going." Through the sobs, she battled to finish each phrase. "I figured he was taking me somewhere to kill me."

"Cate!" Kyle was aghast with the horror. "Oh, honey, I'm so sorry."

Pausing to dry her salt-stained cheeks, she slowly persisted, "He kept hitting me. I was curled up against the locked door, trying to avoid his punches, and he threatened me the whole way. Then he stopped the car, pushed open my door, shoved me out, and sped away. After a moment of lying on the ground, I realized I was at my building."

Kyle examined the apartment door with a flimsy chain and a turn lock on the knob. "Cate, you have to move!" The compounded rage he felt was intense. "It's not safe to be here."

As she shook her head, Cate sought words to describe her emotions. She had lived in terror since that night. "I expected he might come back, but it's been months."

He gripped her hand. "Cate, I have two bedrooms. Move in with me for a while. I insist."

"Kyle, I can't."

"Catie, please. I'm hardly ever even there. I'm always on location or out of town. You'd have the place to yourself. You and Pepper. Come stay with me."

"I can't," she muttered, staring at the floor. "Thank you. Really, I'm okay."

He watched her diminish, sensing she was condemning herself, ravaged by her misplaced guilt. "You know, Cate," he said, squeezing her hand, "none of this was your fault."

"That doesn't matter," she whispered weakly. "Because it feels like it is. I didn't listen to my gut or trust myself."

Kyle lightly wiped the tears from her cheeks with the flat of his hand. There was a long hush as he scrambled for what to say, devoured by an array of brief images of sweet Cate brutalized.

He kissed her forehead and abruptly leaped up.

"Let me get you some water," he called as he rapidly entered her kitchen, glass in hand. He had to break away to absorb the truth. Cate reacted to his sudden departure, her heart breaking at what she perceived as his rejection.

Out of sight, Kyle leaned forward on the sink, hands clutching the sides. His rising anger was palpable. His knuckles were turning white from the strain of his ferocity. He needed to track this guy down and strangle him with his bare hands. Taking slow, deep breaths, attempting to control his rage, he rubbed his eyes, pushing down the pain, preventing the scream in his head from erupting. Time seemed to stand still and rush forward in equal measure. *Wait ... Nana's words ... a friend would be accepting and supportive. I have to think of Cate first.*

With the glass refilled, he returned to the living room. He recognized her devastated expression.

"Have some water. It'll help," he offered kindly. She nodded and took a sip, setting down the glass. He gently drew her to him and embraced her, kissing her head.

"Thanksgiving when we visited Nana, what did she say to you?"

"She told me to hold my head up and be proud of the good person I am. She said no one can rob me of that."

"That's true." He ran his fingers through her hair.

"I certainly don't feel good anymore. I feel pretty broken ... and defective ... damaged."

Her words tore into him. "No, please don't ever say that!" Lovingly, Kyle stroked her head, quieting her fears as new ones formed in him ... what were the right words?

In silence, the search for expression began. Kyle understood her distance, her withdrawal from the people who cared for her. He heard the vacancy in her voice, the echo of pain. He knew in her mind she was haunted. How do you escape such a horrendous experience? He realized she could not bear the rejection she felt for herself. Indeed, what she said about being defective was wrong ... ridiculous even ... but he had to acknowledge her agony. And yet it hurt him that she saw herself somehow mutated. His mind hollered if only he could turn back time.

Forcing down the requirement to take revenge upon the culprit, he tried to unravel what this knowledge meant for him. Compassion, of course, and an ever-increasing need to be by her side. Nothing that she exposed reformed how he felt about her or lessened the stirrings inside him for her. How could he demonstrate his unwavering support without releasing the desperation to tear apart the evil that tried to destroy this beautiful woman? Even though he couldn't divulge his truth—that he undeniably felt so much unquenched desire for her—he still had to show his strength of character.

He reeled; it was his heart he wanted to unchain. The confusion seemed to thwart him. Fighting the need to rescue her and take her far from here, escaping the world's ugliness and miraculously ridding her of this vile incident, he knew the best thing he could do was the simplest—to wrap Cate in his arms, be a faithful friend, and keep her confidence.

"Look at me." He held her chin to gaze into her eyes, ensuring he had her full attention. "You're none of those things. You are ... you're my Cate."

She fell into his arms and felt peaceful, so safe. She never wanted to let go, and neither did he. All that had happened would be their secret, their bond. They remained holding each other until the fullness of the moon bathed the room in soft golden light.

Life would gradually improve. Time, college graduation, lots of work, and companionship made each day hopeful and life a little brighter.

Chapter 23
Edward's Wedding

A few months later, the wretched day arrived on an unseasonably temperate end-of-April morning.

After the ceremony, Joseph and Kyle—dressed in finely tailored suits—waited outside the church door for Cate. Her bridesmaid attire was less than attractive, although she managed to be ravishing.

"You don't look happy," observed Kyle.

"Biggest mistake of my brother's life, and I'm forced to participate. And do you see this dress? Could it be any more hideous?!" Holding her arms out to the sides, she slowly rotated, giving the full effect.

"Yeah, it's some dress," chuckled Joseph. "I'm no fashion expert, but that's just plain ugly. Why did she pick it?"

"She was afraid someone might outshine her on her special day," she scorned.

Without forethought, Kyle said, "You're still the most beautiful woman I … here."

Cate flashed a smile. "Come meet my mom." She skipped on ahead.

Joseph scoffed at Kyle. "You were gonna say the most beautiful woman you know, weren't you?"

"But I didn't," he defended.

Joseph exhaled, disgruntled, following their friend to her mom.

"Mom, I wanna introduce you to Joseph Beason and Kyle Weston."

"Hello, Mrs. Leigh," said Joseph.

Kyle added, "Nice to meet you, ma'am."

"Good to meet you both. So, you're Catherine's acting companions." She was unconsciously fussing with the sleeves of her dress, not gathering what she was saying. "It must be a maddening career, impossible to succeed."

Joseph held back a laugh, and Cate went to correct her mother. Kyle sharply shook his head to keep Cate from saying anything. He found Doris as charming and unassuming as her lovely daughter. "It can be, Mrs. Leigh," he agreed. "It takes a lot of hard work and even more luck."

"It was a nice wedding, wasn't it?" Doris sounded distressfully unsure.

"Yes, it was."

Doris smiled. "Well, have fun. This is costing Edward a bit. We might wish to enjoy it. Nice meeting you, gentlemen." She began to leave and then turned and kissed each on the cheek. "Thank you for being my daughter's friends."

As Doris walked away, Kyle winked at Cate. "You have an affectionate mother."

"Yes, Italian. We kiss everyone." She shook her finger. "Platonic."

Joseph changed the subject. "No more rock concerts, huh? Your brother has a wife to take now."

"Oh, no, you're right! Bad enough I lost my brother to that shrew. Now, no more shows. I love concerts."

"I'll take you, Cate," Kyle energetically offered, igniting yet another deadly death stare from Joseph.

Curtly, an angry voice drew their interest. Valerie was loudly shouting at Edward.

"That's not a promising start," commented Joseph. "She's not very …"

"She's a bitch!" roared Cate.

Both men were surprised. They had never heard her use foul language.

"Then why did he marry her?" Kyle watched as Doris interceded to quell the newlyweds' quarrel.

"Yeah, the sex can't be that good," Joseph sneered, Kyle elbowing him to keep quiet.

"She told him she was pregnant," said Cate.

Joseph was startled. "Is she?"

"No. She lied. Unfortunately, the wedding plans were finalized, and Ed opted to go ahead. I bet she gets pregnant immediately, though."

"And he's paying for it?" he grilled.

"Yep, with the *huge* paycheck he gets for being a young associate starting at the bottom of the law firm." She looked at her brother sympathetically. "Of course, he borrowed ten thousand dollars from me to help pay for this."

"Where did you get that much money to spare?" asked Kyle.

"From my college fund." She tugged at her waistband, twisting it to make it look more presentable.

"You mean money your parents put aside for your education?" Kyle persisted.

Joseph tapped her hand to stop her from tugging at the dress. "You're making it worse."

Frowning at Joseph, Cate huffed, frustrated. "No, it's my money from the commercials I made as a child. I had plenty left over because I completed my studies early."

Kyle was stunned. "You were acting when you were little?"

"Yeah, some local San Diego car commercials for my dad's friend who owned a dealership," she said nonchalantly.

"How old were you when you made these commercials?" he asked.

"Nine until I turned twelve."

"Did you get a union card?"

"Yes, first thing."

Joseph was fascinated. "Kyle, Cate's been in the business longer than us. We were seventeen, remember? She was a seasoned professional before our first audition."

Kyle looked at her curiously. "Why didn't you tell us?"

"You never asked. Anyway, enjoy the reception. You're drinking my childhood acting credits."

Joseph surveyed the circle of women in the open area. "She's throwing the bouquet. You gonna try?"

"No, who'd want her bad luck bouquet anyway! This won't last."

"Such an optimist," jested Joseph.

"Realist." She fidgeted in the ungainly dress. "Ugh, I'm so full of pent-up energy over this. Wanna help me work this off?"

Their eyes widened, and both guys sputtered.

"What?" Cate questioned innocuously. "Surfing. Don't you guys know how to surf?"

"I do," replied Kyle swiftly.

"I don't," Joseph stated. "I can swim, though."

"Let's go and get my board." She stomped away, still pulling at the gangly dress.

Kyle stared at Joseph. "Did you think she meant something other than surfing when she first said …"

"Yes, I did! That girl really needs a bodyguard."

Chapter 24
The Shoot

Manager Tom Jenkins and agent Gabbée Marshall had represented Kyle since his first big break. Cate knew she was in excellent company with their assistance. On a recent audition, she was cast in a substantial supporting role in *Chances Fascination* starring Franky Bankston, one of the highest-paid actors in the business, and well-known actress Lucy Landman, shooting on location in San Francisco. These were the opportunities she had envisioned. She was walking on a cloud. When her phone rang, Joseph shared he was in the same movie. A project with one of her best pals could not have been more ideal.

She would have to wait to tell Kyle the exciting news. He was out of town again. She had lost track of why—publicity, location filming, negotiating a new project. It was hard to tell.

When they arrived at the location, Cate and Joseph hunted for a production assistant to figure out where they should be. The crew was in a tizzy. Something big had happened. An efficient PA hailed them and handed them their call sheets.

"What's going on?" Joseph scanned the area.

"Franky Bankston was rushed to the hospital for emergency surgery."

"Really? Is he okay?" Cate admired Franky's talent and had been eager to meet him.

"Yeah, he'll be fine. Although, he'll be laid up for a while. We had to find a replacement."

"Who?" Joseph asked.

"Kyle Weston. He'll be here any minute."

Looking at each other, they laughed.

※

The first evening, the three visited an Italian restaurant in North Beach.

"When the news came down Franky was hospitalized, the producers called Tom to see if I'd be willing to take on the role. I've wanted this part from the beginning, but they wanted a bigger name—Franky. I feel bad for him. This is a blockbuster role."

"Weren't you committed to another project?" Joseph was unsuccessfully spinning his spaghetti on a fork. Cate stared at him, bothered that he was slopping sauce everywhere.

"The only thing I had going was a guest star role in a new drama. Tom was able to delay it until next season." Kyle sprinkled cheese onto his lasagna.

She handed Joseph a clean spoon. "Use this, please. It's much easier." She demonstrated using her spoon and fork.

"Are you teaching me table manners now?" he asked, colored with sarcasm.

"No, the proper way to eat Italian food. I'm kind of an expert at it."

"You can be a bit of a pest sometimes," he chuckled.

Cate snubbed his wisecrack. "Well, I'll tell you what I'm looking forward to this next month." Her excitement was evident.

"What?" mumbled Joseph with a mouthful of pasta.

"Seeing how you both behave on location. It's gonna be so much fun!"

Joseph and Kyle stared at each other as she sliced into her eggplant parmesan.

"Ah, Cate, ah …" Kyle seemed flustered, passing the grated cheese to Joseph.

"What're *you* like on location, Cate?" interrupted Joseph, getting the hint from his comrade.

"It's my first time," she said. "However, if I were alone, I'd retreat to my hotel room, learn my lines, and sleep. This'll be much more exciting being with you guys."

"Cate, why don't you do that anyway?" began Kyle carefully. "Ya know, study your lines."

"Why?" She sounded hurt. "Don't you want me around?"

"Always. Except Lucy Landman and I have a bit of history."

Setting her arms in front of her on the table, Cate fought her wounded, clouded emotions.

"Fine," she said loftily. "I've seen the covers of tabloids. I'm not blind."

She zeroed in on Joseph, who was seriously diving into his meal, not paying attention.

"And you?"

He glanced up, utterly oblivious. "Great spaghetti."

She exhaled and pushed her barely eaten meal away.

"You guys really stomped on my expectations. I thought we would read lines together, talk about the day's filming, rehearse for the next day …"

"Braid each other's hair," Joseph kidded.

⚜

Cate and Joseph's rooms were on the same floor.

"I guarantee Lucy will be a distraction for Kyle," he said kindly as he walked her to her door.

"I'd imagine you should be focused when you work, not distracted."

"Cate, you're very wise," he heartened.

※

After a long work week, Kyle spending most of his free time with Lucy, the three finally had a chance to get together, a weekend break from filming. The friends were hanging out in Kyle's suite. With the radio on in the background, Cate lounged on the couch, her script tossed to the floor while Kyle read over his, seated on the oversized chair, and Joseph was in a lengthy conversation on the phone.

"Joseph, get off the phone so we can go eat. I'm hungry," she hollered, then addressed Kyle. "He's always on the phone now that he broke up with Marcie. Maybe they'd still be together if he'd talked to *her* more."

Making notes in his script, Kyle smiled, admiring her charm.

The radio station played AC/DC's *You Shook Me All Night Long*. Cate bopped to the music while stretched out on the couch, eyes closed, oblivious of the lyrics she was singing.

She was a fast machine. She kept her motor clean …

Bringing down his script to spy on what she was doing in her musical world, Kyle laughed.

He cleared his throat, "Cate, do you know what this song's about?"

"Ah, cars, or is it dancing?"

"Have you never listened to the words you're singing?"

"Why? Am I singing the boy's part?"

He grinned at her cluelessness. "You live in your own little world, don't you?"

Joseph hung up the phone.

She exhaled loudly. "Finally! I'm famished."

"Sorry, Cate. I've made other plans." Joseph stood at the side of Kyle's chair and tried to be tactful. "Do you have any?"

"Yeah, how many do you need?" Kyle answered inaudibly.

Elongating her neck to better behold what they were doing, she strained to hear.

"A couple." Joseph glanced at Cate to guarantee she couldn't see.

Reaching into his pocket, Kyle took out his wallet and removed something, slipping it to Joseph.

"Here, take three," he mumbled.

"Thanks. I'll see you tomorrow." Turning, Joseph quickly announced, "And Cate, the song's about sex." The door slammed shut.

"It is?!" Her eyes widened. "Ohhh …"

Belly laughing, Kyle returned to his script.

She regrouped her composure.

"So, what was that about?" she queried adamantly, tapping her fingers impatiently.

"What do you mean?"

"You and Joseph. What did he ask for?"

He remained silent.

"What did you give him?" she persisted.

"Condoms, all right? There. See, now you're blushing!"

"Well, I'm honored to be privy to your sex lives," she said dryly, then moaned, "Oh, I need female friends."

"I tried to be subtle."

"Well, it's good to find out you're responsible," she said more maturely.

"Always!"

She narrowed her eyes. "And that means?"

"You just complained you didn't like being privy."

"Now I'm curious." She sat up and stared at him.

"Since my first experience, I've always been prepared and used them."

"Gee, Kyle, you sound like a sex education textbook."

"No, I'm saying I've seen many actors' lives and careers ruined by mistakes." He made notes in his script. "Plus, look at your brother. What happened to your brother won't ever happen to me."

"She wasn't pregnant."

"But it was a believable lie."

"Condoms aren't a hundred percent, Mister Sex Expert." She sagged back down. "Ever think about abstinence?"

"Right, that's a fun concept. You must be the only kid who ever paid attention in health class."

"Yeah, I did." Scanning the ceiling, an idea came to her. "How 'bout we go to the movies?" Grabbing the trades, she paged to movie releases. "Hey! *Terminator 2* opened. We could see that."

"Why? Didn't the first one end the story?"

"I know. I wonder how they'll continue without Reese. He's my favorite character." She stretched while yawning. "I love *The Terminator*. It's the most romantic movie!"

"How's a cyborg coming back in time to snuff out some young woman romantic?" Highlighting one more section of the script, he twirled the pen around.

"It's Reese," Cate said. "He risks his life to save the woman he loves and has never even met." She smiled to herself, reliving the visual experience in her mind.

"Kind of sappy," he snickered.

"It's not," she replied, aggravated. "It's beautiful. I've seen it half a dozen times. Anyway, let me see what time it plays." She read through the showtimes.

Kyle closed his script, setting it down. "Sorry. Not tonight. Another time."

"Fine, I'll take a nap then." She turned to her side, away from him.

"Cate, you have to leave."

She rotated back to face him. "Why?'

"I'm seeing someone tonight."

"Lucy with the bleached blond hair?" she mocked.

"Yes, Lucy."

"Well, I'm not going anywhere. You'll have to cancel your date and hang out with me. I'm comfortable here." She laid back and put her arms behind her head to sleep, shutting her eyes.

Walking up to her, Kyle extended his hand. "Give me your room key."

"Why?" Cate peeked out of one eye.

"You can stay here, and I'll use your room." He opened and closed his hand for the key.

"Oh God, I'm going." She rolled off the couch and scooped up her script. "So harsh!"

She reached the door, turning with a pout. "Make sure you have plenty of condoms, stud."

"Goodnight, Cate. See you tomorrow."

Weeks passed. After a successful shoot for all, Cate attended her first wrap party. A little unsure, she met Kyle at his suite so she wouldn't go alone. He had ended his fling with Lucy a couple of days earlier. Being professional, it didn't seem to faze either one of them.

Kyle yelled for Cate to enter when she knocked on his door. She stepped in dressed in a new form-fitting, sleek black dress and high heels.

"Is this okay for tonight?" she asked timidly.

Preoccupied with finding the room key, Kyle seized his wallet and answered her question before he actually saw her. "Yeah, you look nice …" He glanced up, shocked. "I mean …"

"What? I wasn't sure. It's new." She ran her hands down the sides of the dress. "It's kind of tight. Looks dumb, huh?"

"No, you're dazzling," he said, his mouth falling slightly open, eyes bulging.

He shook his head from the stupor. "Shall we go?"

Joseph and his new girlfriend, Cindy, head of the hotel's guest services, wandered up, sipping their cocktails. Cate nibbled on the shrimp appetizers, seeking other fun foods to pile onto her plate. She had a voracious appetite tonight as she tried to avoid the prying interest of the crew and cast.

"Well, don't you look nice," said Joseph, approvingly.

"Lots of guys eyeing you," Cindy added.

Across the room, Kyle was in a discussion with Lucy, who kept glowering at Cate, having noticed they had arrived together. Cate, Joseph, and Cindy watched the simmering conversation from the appetizer table.

"I guess," Cate surmised, "it wasn't an uneventful breakup like Kyle made it sound."

"Goodness," said Cindy. "I think Lucy doesn't appreciate the competition, Cate."

"I'm not. We're friends," she countered, seeking assurance from her pal. "Right, Joseph?"

Joseph nodded. "Yeah, everybody knows …"

His words were cut short when Lucy slapped Kyle hard across the face and stormed out of the party.

"Whoa!" exclaimed Cindy while Joseph slowly shook his head, and Cate stared in horror.

"Well, that's a good indication she's had enough of Kyle's devil-may-care attitude about relationships," stated Joseph. "Karma, man."

Cindy was tickled. "I need a fresh drink."

"Okay," he agreed.

While Joseph and Cindy headed toward the bar, Cate wandered to the back table where the champagne glasses were being filled.

Kyle strolled up to Joseph and Cindy.

"Need me to get you an ice pack, Kyle?" Cindy suggested.

With an embarrassed expression, he dropped his head. "I do have an interesting effect on women, don't I?"

"What's Lucy's problem? Didn't you lay down the ground rules clear enough?" Joseph pointed out the red handprint on his cheek. Cindy reached into her handbag, pulled out a makeup puff, and dabbed it on Kyle's face.

"There, that's better," she said.

Kyle smiled.

Joseph looked at his empty glass. "We were headed to the bar for another drink. Coming, Kyle?"

"No thanks," he mumbled, noticing Cate standing alone in the back.

As Kyle excused himself and made his way to Cate, Cindy grabbed Joseph's arm.

"I believe Lucy's right in slapping Kyle," she said. "He's in love with Cate."

⁂

Cate scoped the room full of people as the evening wore on. She looked down at her dress and straightened the fabric. It was definitely tight. *Is it supposed to fit like this?* The men in the room kept staring at her. She was feeling increasingly on display.

Moving her attention to the filled champagne glasses lining the table, Cate admired the costly labels on the bottles.

She wondered how does expensive champagne taste? It had to be better than a five-dollar bottle her mom would buy for the holidays. She was tempted to sneak a sip. Glancing around carefully, she picked up a glass and then changed her mind, setting it down.

"I saw that." The voice startled her.

She swung around. "Hi, Kyle."

140

"Don't worry. I won't tell anybody," he said with a mischievous grin. "Anyway, as far as they're concerned, you could be twenty-five years old, not twenty. They don't know." He picked up a glass.

"Do I look twenty-five?" she asked excitedly.

"No," he laughed, "you barely look like you're sixteen, baby face."

Cate's enthusiasm crashed.

"One day," he continued, oblivious of his unintentional insult, "you'll appreciate looking so young."

"Maybe."

Deciding to forgive Kyle for the slight, she glanced back at the full glasses. "I've never had real champagne."

Kyle handed her his glass. "Go ahead. Try it. No one's watching."

She peeped around—everyone was caged in their storytelling. She sipped it quickly. It tickled her nose, and she giggled, handing it back.

"Good?" he inquired.

She nodded fervidly.

"So, your girlfriend looked upset," Cate said. "Everything okay with Lucy?"

"Lucy was never my girlfriend. She was … just sex."

"Not surprising she slapped you." The words flew from her mouth, causing her to lower her eyes; she realized she may have hurt him. "Oh. Sorry, Kyle. I didn't mean that."

"No problem." He still seemed uncomfortable.

Looking about the room, Kyle viewed the crowd milling around and reached for his champagne glass to take another sip, offering it to her.

"No, thanks. One sip to see what it was like." She picked up her purse. "I guess I should get back. I need to pack. I have an early flight in the morning."

He set the glass down and took her hand. "Why don't we share a ride to the hotel?"

Chapter 25
1992

The prior year, 1991, had been relatively busy for Cate, gaining more and better supporting roles. She had a flair for comedy; her timing was impeccable. She even made a series pilot. It wasn't picked up. However, Cate was a known talent, and casting directors and many producers often requested her directly for a small role without auditioning.

Joseph had landed a regular role in a medical drama. At least he filmed in L.A., spending time with her during short breaks.

On the other hand, Kyle was gone more often than in town. He was now a major star. If Cate missed a call from him—which unfortunately happened quite often—she could always read about his activities standing at the checkout counter.

It was her friendship with Julia that kept her grounded. Julia reminded her constantly that she had a tremendous future.

With college behind her, Cate spent evenings and weekends at the movies to fill her free moments. Movies were her happy place. She tried to avoid Kyle's films, though. Seeing his movies alone left her with an aching emptiness.

On occasion, she would sneak past the Malibu privacy fence to view the elegant beach house she and Kyle had found. Her imagination ran wild.

Chapter 26
Happy 21st

Joseph shuddered as he watched Cate slurp down a dozen raw oysters.

"Cate, I love ya, hon, but that's disgusting."

"You don't eat raw oysters. I get it. But don't begrudge me my celebration. It's my birthday, and I'm enjoying them." She rotated the oyster tray to get to the uneaten ones.

"And you're twenty-one! We can finally go to the bars without sneaking you in." Joseph sat back to distance himself from Cate's meal.

After sprinkling Tabasco sauce onto the last few oysters, she lifted his glass, grimacing at the smell. "Ewe, scotch. I like soda. So, who's coming to this little shindig? I thought you'd bring your new girlfriend."

"Sorry, Lilly had to work." He took a swig of his drink. "But Julia and John should be here any minute. Kyle's out of town."

"I didn't expect him." She scooped out the last oyster.

He made an effort to pacify the hurt he sensed she felt. "Kyle really did want to be here to celebrate your birthday."

"I envy him working this much. I envy you, too. For each job I get, you get three." Swallowing the oyster, her eyes grew big, and she chugged her water.

He screwed up his face. "Too much hot sauce?"

Nodding, she waved her hand in front of her mouth. Joseph handed her his water, which she immediately gulped.

"Thank you," she laughed, pushing away the empty oyster tray.

"Anyway," he smiled, getting back to the subject. "Us working more often than you. I know it seems unfair."

"No, don't get me wrong. I'm proud of you. Both of you."

A notion—the image of where Kyle was and with whom, caused her to retract. Joseph had a striking instinct when it came to Cate.

"The woman doesn't mean anything to him."

She glimpsed up. "Who're you referring to?"

"The model with him on the cover of *Movie Inquiry*. Ya know what I'm talkin' about. Those pictures are photoshopped, anyway," he deflected earnestly.

"Hey, like you and Lilly, I wish him happiness."

Joseph exhaled a tentative breath. "Kyle's not that happy."

"How can't he be? He's a celebrity. A major movie star. He's in demand with the studios. Everybody loves him." Again, her mind drifted to the woman on the tabloid cover with Kyle.

He gazed at her with empathy and sighed, "Yeah."

"Happy Birthday, Cate!" Julia scurried to the table, tugging John along with her. "Ooh, oysters. I'm getting two dozen raw for John and me." She motioned to the server, indicated Cate's tray, and held up two fingers.

"Please, no!" groaned Joseph. "Now I know I'm gonna be sick."

"Cate, where's your cocktail?" asked John. "You can drink now."

"Most liquor tastes pretty nasty to me, and I hate beer."

"Except she loves champagne," Joseph asserted.

"So I hear," grinned Julia.

The server set down the two oyster trays in front of the group.

"No worries." Julia turned to the server. "Hi, it's my friend's birthday. May we get her a glass of Veuve Clicquot demi-sec? Thanks. You'll love it, Cate." She squeezed fresh lemons on the oysters, feeding John the first one.

"What were you two discussing before we rudely interrupted?"

she added. "You seemed pretty serious."

"Kyle's unhappiness," remarked Joseph.

"Why's he unhappy?" asked John, unwrapping a cracker to eat with the oysters.

"Exactly," Julia goaded. "He's a millionaire!"

They all stared at Joseph for the answer. "Why're you looking at me?" He then noticed something straight ahead and pointed. "Ask him yourself."

"Happy Birthday, Catie!" Everyone turned toward Kyle's voice. Cate quaked with excitement. "What're you doing here?!"

"I scheduled a couple of days off. I couldn't miss your big birthday." He set down a bottle of Dom Pérignon with a large bow on it.

"Oh no! You're not upstaging my gift," Julia said as she set the bottle aside. "Take this home, Cate, and save it for another occasion."

The conversation was uplifting. After buying Cate yet another glass of champagne, Julia and John shared their wedding plans for mid-September. Kyle disclosed details on his upcoming project, and Joseph brought up specifics of his recent episode. Although Cate laughed and listened keenly, she said little. She was tied to watching everyone else's interactions, especially Kyle.

Carrying out a birthday cake Julia had brought, covered in twenty-one candles, the waiter set it down in front of Cate. She was ecstatic.

"Make this a good wish, Cate," Julia encouraged. "It's a milestone."

Closing her eyes, Cate envisioned herself in Kyle's embrace. Blushing, she blew out the candles. Again, she stole a glimpse at Kyle ... all she wanted was him.

At the end of the evening, Cate walked toward Joseph's car to get a ride home. He was in a huddle with Kyle.

Reclining against the passenger door, she patiently waited. Feeling loopy, she held the Dom in one hand and held onto the car with the other to steady herself. Her head was spinning. Two glasses of champagne were far too much for her first drinking binge on a stomach with raw oysters and a couple of bites of birthday cake.

"Hey, Cate, I have to stop at Lilly's. Do you mind if Kyle drives you home?"

"No, not at all. Thank you, Joseph, for tonight. It was so much fun."

"Take care, Cate." Joseph hugged her, and over her shoulder, he looked at Kyle and mouthed, *behave!*

She laid her head on the headrest in the car and breathed through her mouth. "I guess I should've eaten more than oysters. But I sure liked the champagne. I think I prefer demi-sec to brut. It was delicious."

"Yeah, you kinda drank it like water," Kyle said. "Sorry about my present … the Dom's brut."

"That was nice of you. You're always so thoughtful. Thank you. I'll save it for my next birthday." She paused. "Do people get used to drinking? Because this could be embarrassing if I'm snockered on one or two drinks."

She closed her eyes and took quelling, methodical breaths, listening to Whitesnake on the radio.

Is this love, or am I dreaming …

Kyle observed her affectionately, fighting his weaker nature.

As he walked her to her apartment, she abruptly stopped when she came to the staircase.

"What's wrong?" he asked.

She scowled at the stairs as if they were an enemy. "I can't climb those."

"Well, you can't camp-out down here."

Her vision was a bit fuzzy. She attempted a simper and clutched Kyle's arm, supporting her wobbly legs. He picked her up and carried her up the stairs to her door.

"Are you carrying me over the threshold?" She flirted, "How romantic."

"Stop it," he laughed.

Snuggling in his arms, she handed her keys to him. It was clumsy to hold her and unlock the door simultaneously.

Once inside, he kicked closed the door and took her to the bedroom, gently laying her on the bed.

"Thank you," she said faintly.

"You need anything, birthday girl? Maybe something to eat?"

Slowly shaking her head, she recalled Joseph's comment—*Kyle's not that happy.*

"What?" he quietly asked.

"Are you happy?"

"Am I happy? Why do you ask?"

She opened her eyes broadly, a longing on her face. "I ..." She had a gnawing—*I could make you happy.* She could never be so brazen.

"What is it, beautiful?" He brushed back her hair.

"You're the best birthday present. I mean, coming to my birthday. Thank you."

Kyle felt the smoldering inside.

"I could never miss my favorite girl's birthday." Captivated by her alluring brown eyes, he felt beckoned, a warm ache overtaking him. He stopped. "Hey, I've gotta go."

She clutched his hand. "Don't leave."

"Cate," he warned, realizing this was a dangerous convergence.

"Please stay." Her breathing was shallow, desirous.

The craving intensified. It would be effortless to give in and pull her to him.

"Kyle, it *is* my birthday."

"I know." Tenderly, he ran his fingers through her hair.

"I'm not a little girl. I'm a woman. Please."

Her look was inviting and unassuming, just like their first trip to Malibu, lying back on the dune, the sun low in the sky–the day she asked him for time, not being ready for love …

He stroked her cheek. "You have the face of an angel. The champagne went to your head. You don't know what you're saying."

"I do. Don't you wan …" She looked down sadly, rejected.

Undoubtedly, he did. He never wanted anything more. Leaning forward, his lips so near hers, her expression breathtakingly innocent. He pulled away.

"I have to go." Being strong for them, Kyle kissed Cate on the forehead and sighed.

He was gone.

Chapter 27
Perfect Fit

Summer passed. Besides improving their overall careers, the months went by quickly and uneventfully.

※

The group showed up for an after-five evening on Labor Day weekend. It had been a while since Kyle had seen them, having just arrived from a location shoot.

He sat next to Cate at the table, with John sitting to her left and Julia and Joseph across from them. The theme was directed at Julia and John's impending nuptials.

"Everyone's bringing dates?" Julia asked efficiently. "I'm confirming my headcount for the caterer."

"I'm bringing Lilly," remarked Joseph. "She's excited about coming and is driving me nuts over what she's gonna wear."

"You two are getting' pretty serious, Joseph," Julia gleamed.

"Whoa ... well, maybe."

Julia made a speedy note in her wedding planner, which she carried everywhere.

"How 'bout you, Cate?"

"I don't know anybody," she answered casually, munching on the cocktail peanuts.

Kyle studied her and said nothing.

"Kyle?" Julia pursued, tapping her pen repeatedly.
"To be determined," he quickly muttered.
"John, your friends?"
"You have my list, sweetheart. But you can scratch Lenny from it. He was in a fender bender and is laid up for a while."
"Is he okay?" she asked, crossing his name off the list.
"Yeah, he'll be fine, but he can't attend. Oh, Cate, it reminds me. Did you ever get a settlement from your friend's insurance company for the car accident?"
Cate's expression grew distant. "Ah, no, I never filed a claim."
"Damn, Cate. At least you should have gotten some money for your pain and suffering," said Joseph. "Whatever happened to your friend who was driving?"
Kyle silently watched her as she strived to make light of the event.
She stammered, her eyes fixating on her napkin. "She … um … left town. I heard she's in Las Vegas."
As Cate placed her hands on her lap, Kyle subtly held them reassuringly. Her eyes met his for a brief spell of connection. It touched her, giving her strength.
Julia calculated the exchange between them, swiftly returning the topic to the wedding.
"Well, it's too late to reduce the headcount, so you must recruit someone to bring, Cate. I hate wasting food."
The rest of the gathering was lively, ending with Julia asking Cate, a bridesmaid, to attend her final wedding dress fitting later in the week.

The seamstress meticulously pinned the hemline. Standing before the mirror, Julia modeled the flowing gown.
"Cate, what do you think?" Julia readjusted to study the garb from every angle.

Touching her chest with her hand, Cate took an excited breath. "Oh Julia, you look incredible!"

"You like it?" She glimpsed over her shoulder, the seamstress tugging at the fabric to lengthen it.

"I love it," said Cate. "You're a fairy princess."

"Aren't they supposed to be pure?" Julia laughed, "The white dress's a fashion statement. I'm not that innocent."

The seamstress stepped out to the backroom, and Julia motioned for Cate to come closer.

"Okay, speaking of pure …"

"Yes?"

Julia hounded, "Well? Are you still?"

"If you're asking that horrible, invasive question again …" Cate forcibly breathed out with aggravation. "No, I haven't been with anyone. Why do you care so much?"

"Well, I'm concerned you're giving it too much importance. You're an adult."

"That's not what I've been told." She plunked down on the divan and sipped her bottled water.

"You're a woman. It's probably time, for goodness' sake."

Pointing at the water, Cate walked over to share the bottle. "It might help if there was someone in my life."

"True." Julia meddled, "Don't you wanna date?"

"Date? Yeah, maybe. But I won't sleep around! No, I was raised to believe you saved yourself for someone special."

"Cate, this is 1992, not 1952."

"Julia, it means something to me." Her mind flashed to Kyle.

"I'm introducing you to a funny guy named Brady, one of John's co-workers." She slid on long white gloves to see how they'd look with the gown. "He's adorable, too. He'll be at the wedding. I'll set it up."

"Please don't," whimpered Cate.

"What're you waiting for? Or maybe I should ask, who're you waiting for?" she spurred perceptively, staring at her bridesmaid mutely slouched forward. "Cate, you'll wait forever, sweetie. He sees you as a kid. And for all his flaws, Kyle's a decent guy. He won't take advantage. Anyway, you don't wanna be a part of his harem. And frankly, sex screws up a friendship. No, you need to look for a nice ordinary guy."

Julia sat beside her and clutched her hand. "Where's my cheerful Cate?"

"I'm cheerful," she defended.

"Not like you used to be. You're ... I don't know, different. You seem lonely."

"I'm not lonely. I have you and Joseph."

Julia acknowledged her friend was not going to admit her anxieties.

"And you always will." She stood up and looked into the mirror. "So, this is good?"

"Julia, you look awesome!"

Chapter 28
A Southern Gentleman

It was a glorious September afternoon, Julia and John's wedding day. Cate was determined to arrive early in case the perfectionist bride needed her assistance to get ready.

Rushing to get to the church, she climbed into her car. Her bridesmaid dress came slightly below her knees, extraordinarily sexy and tight-fitting. Julia chose a bridesmaid dress a woman would definitely use more than once. Lifting her foot into the car, her high heel scraped against her nylons on the opposite leg, running them and tearing a hole atop her foot. There was no way to hide this rip. She needed another pair of pantyhose.

Tracking down a shop in an area she'd be driving past to get to the church might be impossible. She had to stop at the first drugstore she spotted. Running in, she was relieved to discover they had pantyhose and stood in line, antsy to get on the road.

"Aren't you a little overdressed for shopping?" A voice behind her carried a slight southern accent. She turned to see a handsome man in his mid-twenties with sandy-colored hair and green eyes grinning at her. He was dressed in a classic Brooks Brother suit.

"Aren't you?" she replied.

"Left a business meeting."

Cate gestured to her dress. "On my way to a wedding."

"Bridesmaid?"

She nodded, placing her notice on the nylons she held, her

shyness rearing its head.

"My, does your friend who's getting married know you'll steal the show?" He friskily smiled, making her feel more at ease.

"Thanks, but she's stunning." She blushed, "I doubt I'll be stealing anything."

"Not true," he glinted wily. "You've already stolen my heart."

His personality quite took her as she made her purchase. After quickly paying for his cola, he walked her to her car.

"I have to go. I can't be late," said Cate, swiftly unlocking the car door.

Tapping her shoulder, he asked, "Wait, I'm here for a couple of days. What're you doing after the wedding?"

"Hanging out with my friends."

Reclining against her car's side, he coyly smiled. "May I join you?"

"You're a stranger," she said warily.

"I'd like to remedy that," he enticed. "Sorry, I'm sure you're always getting hit on. And judging where we are, I imagine the guys out here are smooth." He humbly added, "I swear I'm a simple southern boy. No bad intent. Merely would like to talk with you, preferably not in a strip-mall parking lot."

A clever idea came to her. "Come to the wedding."

"Really?"

"Why not? The bride told me to bring a guest," said Cate gallantly. "Besides, you're appropriately dressed."

"Yes! I'd love to! Oh, wait." Putting out his hand to shake, he introduced himself. "I'm Alex Miller from Montgomery, Alabama."

Taking his hand, she was charmed. "Alabama? All I know about that place is Lynyrd Skynyrd's song."

"It's a scenic state with real, decent people. Our children are well-mannered, ma'am." He pretended to bear a hat and tip it to her.

She was pleasantly dazed when he held her vision, Alex's eyes filled with attraction. "I'm ... I'm Catherine Leigh. California girl."

Coming back to reality, she glimpsed the time on her watch. "Oh my gosh, I'm late." She carefully got into the car.

"Great, I'll follow you to the church."

"Stay close. I drive fast."

Kyle and Joseph sat in the pews waiting for the wedding to begin. Joseph had brought his girlfriend, Lilly, and Kyle was attending alone.

For all the planning and headaches and short tempers, the wedding went off without a snag. It was flawless.

After the ceremony, the guests went to the canopied outdoor reception area at the top of the hill. Kyle stood in a group with Joseph and Lilly. He had a glass of champagne to give Cate when she met up with them.

"Why's Pepper at Nana's?" asked Joseph, making conversation.

"She mentioned she's been lonely lately. So, I said she could keep him for a while."

"It's hard not to get attached to the little guy, but I think she was saying you should visit more often," Joseph wisely counseled.

As Cate glided down the path, she appeared more radiant to Kyle than ever. When she reached the group, he handed her the glass.

Accepting his thoughtful gesture, Cate glowed, "Thank you."

"It was a wonderful wedding, wasn't it, Cate?" gushed Lilly.

"Yes! It was moving ... lovely."

Kyle leaned close to tell Cate how beautiful she looked when a strange voice intruded.

"I knew it! You stole the show just like you stole my heart." Alex strutted up with his hand on his chest.

Cate pulled away from Kyle and dashed to Alex. Taking hold of his left hand, she led him to the group.

Joseph looked apprehensive, while Kyle seemed like someone had sucker-punched him.

"Everyone, this is Alex Miller from Montgomery, Alabama. I invited him to the wedding. Show him some California hospitality."

There was an extended lull, gaping, the two men seeing Alex still holding Cate's hand.

"Hi, Alex. I'm Joseph Beason, a friend of Cate's." Joseph extended his hand to shake. "And this is my girlfriend, Lilly."

The delay was excruciatingly drawn out with Kyle, Joseph prompting him to speak. "Kyle."

"Oh, yes." He wrenched himself from his stupor. "Sorry. Kyle Weston."

"The actor Kyle Weston?" Alex was impressed.

Recognizing his friend was visibly shaken, Joseph countered, "The one and only."

"Well, I'm a big fan."

Staring blankly at Alex, Kyle muttered, "Thanks." Then he sternly faced Cate. "May I talk to you for a minute?" Rather brutishly, Kyle swiped her hand from Alex's and whisked her over to the side.

"Who's that dude?"

"Someone I met at a drugstore when I was buying pantyhose. I had a run in my nylons and had to …"

"You picked up some guy at a store?!" he barked, trying to keep his voice down.

"I didn't pick him up." She felt insulted. "We talked, and he seemed nice. He's in town for a few days. I thought, why not bring him?"

"That's the definition of picking up someone." His look burrowed through her.

Recognizing his misplaced irritation, Cate felt superior. "Why are you so bent out of shape? Where's your latest fling? Busy shooting a centerfold?"

"I'm here alone."

"Well," she said breezily, "I'm not."

He grasped the glass from her hand and deposited it on a nearby table. "You're not hanging out with some stranger from Alabama or any other damn State. He could be a serial killer, for all you know. I won't allow it."

"And when," she fiercely berated, "did you become my father?"

"I'm looking out for you," he sputtered indecisively.

"How considerate," she said irreverently. "I'll be fine."

Retrieving her glass, she strutted away.

<hr />

While Cate and Kyle scuffled off to the side, Lilly brought Alex to the main table and introduced him to the bride and groom. The four were having a merry chat and getting along well when Cate wandered up, Kyle having returned to Joseph. Both men were watching as Alex bowed and kissed her hand.

Joseph put his hand on Kyle's shoulder. "You can't have it both ways, ya know. Someone's gonna steal her away. It's inevitable. She's …"

"Perfect," pined Kyle.

<hr />

The reception in full swing, the band's music was rocking, and twinkling lights shone around the canopy as the sun began to set. The mood was joyous and romantic.

After almost two hours of music, festivities, and scowling at Alex, Kyle couldn't tolerate Cate laughing and spending time with the new guy for a moment longer. He marched over to the bench where they were eating wedding cake.

She brought her champagne glass to her lips for a sip, and Kyle snatched the glass from her hand, dumping it in the grass.

"Hey," she snapped, setting her plate down.

Kyle spoke to Alex. "Excuse us." He grabbed her hand. "Let's dance."

He tugged her to the pavilion. "Stop drinking. You can't hold your liquor."

"I haven't even had half a glass. What's that, like three sips?" She wriggled to walk in her tight dress at Kyle's fast pace.

"That's plenty." He pulled her against him to step to the band's slow dance cover of Journey's *Open Arms*.

Lecturing her between flowing moves and spins, he gruffly stated, "I'm driving you home."

"Why? I have my car."

"You've been drinking."

"Three sips," she said, riled. "You poured out the rest. This isn't like my birthday."

"Yeah, your birthday," he droned, a ring of regret.

"You're acting goofy."

"I'll bring you back tomorrow, and you can get your car." He twirled her. The energy between them was intense.

"No, Alex and I are meeting for breakfast. I'll need my car."

He clutched her firmly. "*Meeting* for breakfast?"

"Yes! What're you implying?"

"Nothing," he grunted. "I don't like him."

"You don't have to." Pushing away, she straightened her dress. "Thank you for the dance. And I'm driving myself." She walked assertively to Alex.

Incensed, Kyle stormed out of the reception to his car. He turned on the ignition and turned up the radio to drown out his thoughts. It did not soothe his mood that *Don't Tell Me You Love Me* by Night Rangers was blasting out his speakers. With his hand choking the gearshift, he could not wrap his mind around what was happening. He felt flushed, his head spinning with dubiety. Cold sweat poured from his forehead. He rubbed his scalp roughly, eyes squeezed closed, forcibly attempting to remove the picture of the two of them from his mind. He was teenage jealous and didn't care.

When he opened his eyes again, he observed the southerner walking his dearest friend to the car. Getting her door, Alex inclined into the driver's lowered window. Kyle craned his neck to see if Alex was kissing her. He couldn't tell.

She drove away. Less than a minute later, Alex got into his rental and drove in the same direction. Rattled, Kyle put his car in gear and floored it, heading straight to Cate's, now driven by the tempo of Night Rangers' tune.

There was a pounding on her door. Scared, Cate peeked through the peephole. Kyle? She cracked the door open. "Kyle, what're you doing here?"

"I was making sure you got home safely since you'd been drinking."

"Geez, are you still on the three-sip thing?" She stood aloof with her hands behind her back.

"May I come in?" He stretched his neck to view the inside of her apartment, Fleetwood Mac's *Songbird* romantically filling the air. He had the compulsion to charge into her bedroom to hunt for Alex.

"Sure," she said, trying to subdue her crossness with him.

Cate had changed into shorts and a Tom Petty concert tee-shirt. It was oversized and ridiculously sexy, covering the fact she was wearing shorts.

"What's up?"

"Cate, I ..." Swallowing hard, he had difficulty breathing, feeling weak in the knees. "May I sit down?"

"Yeah, Kyle, you don't look good." Suddenly, she was genuinely troubled. "Are you feeling okay?'

Gingerly, he sat on the sofa and rotated to lie down, flushed and dizzy. "No, actually, I don't."

She touched his forehead with her cool hand. "Kyle, you're burning up."

Running to the bedroom and bathroom, she returned with a pillow and wet washcloth. She put the pillow behind his head, covered him with the throw, and placed the washcloth on his forehead. She then went to the kitchen, poured some fresh juice, and handed him the glass with a handful of vitamins and aspirin.

"Take these."

Removing his shoes so he could stretch out on the sofa, she sat with him for a while, wiping his feverish head with the washcloth. He studied her movements without comment.

"Get some rest," she said softly. "If you need me, I'll be in the bedroom." She adjusted his covers and sweetly palmed his cheek. Shutting off the CD deck, she went to her bedroom.

The silence underscored Kyle's astonishment as he stared in the direction she traveled to her room. He had come here to scold her, win her, possess her—to love her.

Chapter 29
Chicken Soup

Kyle awoke at the door click. Cate was sneaking into the apartment with a shopping bag full of groceries.

"I'm sorry," she said. "I tried not to wake you. I went out and bought ingredients for my homemade chicken soup. It'll make you better by tomorrow."

"Tomorrow? Cate, I have to go home." He flinched as he forced himself to sit up on the sofa.

"Pepper's with Nana, right?"

"Yes, but I've got a fitting tomorrow morning at the studio." He slowly tried to rise.

Setting the bag on the kitchen counter, she scurried to the sofa to sit beside him. "You're not going anywhere." She gently pushed him back down onto the sofa and covered him again. "I can run to your house and bring back some clean clothes. You can't be comfortable in a fancy suit."

He smiled at her mindfulness. "No need. There's a suitcase in the trunk of my car. I never took it out from my last trip. There should be plenty of clothes in there. Anyway, wouldn't it be easier for me to go home?"

"No way. I'm not sleeping at your house to take care of you. Your place has a tawdry history," she giggled. "No, you're staying here."

"Cate ..." he said, holding her hand.

She pointed towards her room. "Why don't you get in my bed? It's closer to the bathroom and much more comfortable. You'll get better rest. I'll sleep on the sofa."

"No, I'm not throwing you out of your bedroom," he sulked.

"We could ..." Her eyes met his, and she cut off her words. Kyle burned to hear her whole idea. He knew what it was. When it was apparent she wasn't completing the proposal, he spoke, "The sofa's fine."

She smiled and stepped into the kitchen to prepare the soup.

※

The delicious fragrance of the chicken soup wafted into the living room, tempting him. He may be sick, but his appetite had perked up.

Cate was in the back putting up laundry.

"Hey," he yelled, "is the soup ready yet?"

"A few more minutes," she said, exiting the bedroom. "Are you hungry?"

"Yes, I am."

With the small purse she had used the day before at the wedding, she removed a piece of paper and began writing in her notebook, sitting by her answering machine.

He watched her curiously. "What're you doing?"

"Putting Alex's information in my address book."

Kyle put his hands behind his head. "Oh, he left. Good."

"No, he's in town. We exchanged numbers just in case." She skipped over to him. "Look, this is how they abbreviate Birmingham on an address label. *B'ham.* Isn't it cute?"

"Adorable," he snorted. "I thought he lived in ..."

"Montgomery," she completed. "He does. This is his parents' address. He said he travels a lot, and it would be better to write to him there."

She concluded writing in the book and strutted back toward the kitchen.

"Sure, I'm betting he lives with a girlfriend," he snarled. "Or wife. He's shrewdly being careful so she won't find out about you."

"You're a cynic, aren't you? Not all guys are sleazes. He's nice and polite. A gentleman."

"Yeah, right," he bellyached, pulling the blanket to his chin with a beaten look.

She tasted the soup and smiled in approval. "Soup's ready. Do you want pastina or rice in it?"

"What's pastina?" he asked.

"Italian baby pasta, yummy." She walked out of the kitchen, holding the box of pasta up for him to see.

"Okay, whatever the chef recommends."

※

The soup was the most scrumptious meal he could remember. Of course, he was sick, and the fact it made him feel better may have caused his overblown praise.

"Cate, this soup's fantastic. I'm cured. You should bottle this to be a remedy for the common cold."

"I don't think you have a cold," she called from her room. "Body aches?"

"Yes. Why?"

Striding out of the bedroom dressed in the sleek, form-fitting black dress she had purchased for her first wrap party, Cate felt his forehead. "It's the flu that's going around."

"Where're you going?" Kyle sat up, gawking. "Is there a party I wasn't invited to?"

"No, I'm having dinner with Alex since I canceled breakfast this morning." She opened her clutch purse to check for keys.

"I'm glad you're better. Now I can go out for a bit. I'll be back soon. Keep drinking the soup."

"Cate, you shouldn't leave me alone in this condition," he advised without delay, trying for a believable groan.

"Don't be a baby." She gracefully strolled to the door. "You can survive without me." Closing the door, he heard her footsteps trailing away.

"No, I can't."

Chapter 30
The Other Man

The restaurant was classically low-key and renowned for its excellent cuisine. Alex poured more wine into his glass.

"This is fabulous," Cate bashfully said.

"My father recommended it. He's a professional chef. He worked at one of the finest restaurants in Atlanta before moving our family to Birmingham to open his establishment."

She recited the words for *Sweet Home Alabama* in her head to grasp where he lived. Birmingham was mentioned.

"But you live in Montgomery now? Is it different from Birmingham?" She broke off a piece of bread from the basket to sample.

"It's smaller." He passed her the butter, which she politely declined. "There's not much to do, but being there for my job's important. It's the epicenter of government in Alabama."

"Government?"

"I'm a management consultant." Taking some bread for himself, he buttered it. "My clients are mostly government agencies."

"What's management consulting?" She tipped her head.

Nibbling on his bread, he broke down the details of his work. "I evaluate and strategize performance improvement for companies and agencies. I manage people and their skills. I work with everyday people. They're not like you."

She was mystified. "What am I?"

"Special. I mean, you're making a living using your talents. Unique to do what you love and get paid for it." He reached for another slice of bread.

"Yeah." She took a sip of water to hide her lack of sophistication. Dating was challenging. She felt almost graceless.

"Let me ask you," he said, "have you been in anything I might've seen?"

How she hated that question. It was as if she had to audition for the asker to prove she was an actor. In her opinion, it was a rude inquiry, similar to demanding a surgeon show you a removed appendix as proof of a medical degree. Still, she could forgive Alex.

"Possibly. I did a national cola commercial, and there's a movie coming out this fall, *Girls' Break*." She straightened the napkin on her lap. "Juvenile title. It's about girls partying during Spring Break. Oh, and I was in *Chances Fascination*."

"Wasn't that a Weston film?"

"Yeah, Kyle starred in it."

"Is that how you ended up with the part?"

Again, Cate thought the probe a bit presumptuous. "No, I was cast in it way before him."

Slowly, Alex rotated his glass of wine. "It must be interesting being around famous people like Weston."

"Kyle's such a dear friend." Her feelings were uncovered inadvertently; her face seemed to glow as she spoke of him. "He's not famous to me. He's just Kyle."

Bringing the glass to his lips, Alex explored her expression. "Wasn't he voted *Sexiest Man Alive*?"

She smiled. "One of his many, many magazine covers."

Alex raked at her reaction. "He's extremely invested in your life and what you do, don't you think?" He took a long sip.

"He's my best friend," she explained.

"Sure, except he acts like you're his girlfriend. Seems awfully possessive."

"Oh, no," she nervously laughed. "Kyle has a million women he dates. He's just a little protective of me. I mean, he's known me since I was eighteen. I was pretty green then."

Studying her, Alex wisely decided to ward off further interrogation. He turned his concentration to courting her, thinking she would be quite the trophy—the movie star's girl.

Sharing his circuitous occupational trek, he talked non-stop for the entire meal. She stayed quiet, weighing his zest and wondering if everyone from the South was this down-to-earth. It was refreshing from what she experienced daily in Hollywood, where both men and women were invested in their personal dramas, and other people became useful trusses to bolster their careers. Cate allowed long ago how lucky she was to have two friends who were not the Hollywood norm.

"This may be somewhat soon," Alex said languidly. "I'd like you to come to Birmingham and meet my folks. You'd love Alabama."

"You want me to meet your parents? I'm a stranger."

He held her hand. "Not true. I've never felt this close to someone before. You're the most wonderful girl I've met. And I'd be a chump to let you go. May I visit you again if you won't return to Alabama with me?"

Startled, she said guardedly, "Sure. It'd be fun."

"Perhaps next month?" he persevered.

"I'm actually on location next month." Not true as far as she knew, yet the words tumbled from her.

"May I visit you there? Being in an exotic location with you would be exciting," he wooed.

"I'm sorry, I can't. I'm exceptionally focused when I work. I'm too busy to socialize." Also, as Joseph and Kyle would attest, not true.

He realigned his tactics. "I understand. I'll just have to enjoy these hours of being with you until I fly home the day after tomorrow. I have conference meetings in the morning. Perhaps we could have a late lunch or early dinner?"

"Okay. I've got an audition at 9:30. It should be over by noon."

"It's a date, then. Some more wine?" He topped off his wine goblet and reached over with the bottle to do the same with hers.

Cate slid her hand over the top of her glass. "Oh no, thank you. I have to drive home."

He pursued with gentleness in his voice, "No, you don't." Now, he'd close the deal. "I'm staying at this hotel."

"Ahh," she stuttered.

He realized he was about to be shot down. New play…

"I'm sorry, it was ill-mannered of me. I can see you're a nice girl. Please forgive me." He kissed her hand. "You can't fault me. You're beautiful."

Suddenly needing a breather, she balked, nicking her hand from his, and pushed from the table. "Excuse me. I should find the powder room."

His sight followed her as she passed the bar to the restroom. His vision stopped. An attractive woman with flaming red hair flashed him a seductive smile. Alex had seen her at the conference and nodded in response. Handing the waiter his card for the tab, he said, "That woman over there, find out what she's drinking and add it to my bill. Tell her I'm buying her a drink."

When the waiter spoke to her, she fluttered her attention his way, and he winked at her.

Cate returned to the table a few minutes later. The waiter handed back Alex's credit card.

"Ready?" She was impatient to check on Kyle.

"Yes, I'll see you out."

She walked on, Alex hanging back.

"I'll be back in a minute," he said cunningly to the woman at the bar.

At least there was one redhead he could bed tonight.

※

Listening to the Dodgers play the Giants did not distract Kyle from staring at the clock, wondering where Cate was. Or, more specifically, what she was doing. When he heard the clicking of high heels on the walkway and the key in the lock, he quickly shut off the radio and picked up a book on the side table, pretending to read.

Cate smiled as she entered. "Still awake?"

"Your soup has an energizing effect."

"You look much better than yesterday." She sat beside him on the sofa and touched his forehead. She was close enough that his senses were filled with her subtle perfume. It made him a little light-headed to be near her.

"No fever," she reported.

"How was your date?" He closed the book, returning it to the side table.

"Okay."

Frowning, Kyle tried to decipher her appearance. He sensed confusion in her eyes. "Did something happen?"

She set her lungs to tackle a touchy subject that had bothered her most of her young adult life.

"Why, even the nicest guys—why do they expect me, or any woman, to go to bed with them, especially the first night?"

Kyle froze, wordless at first. "Did he do …"

"No, he asked me up to his room."

"And you didn't?"

"Of course I didn't!" she griped, annoyed. "It'd been such an enjoyable evening up until then. I was actually insulted. I felt like I was a piece of meat."

Relieved, Kyle stifled a laugh. "He has no finesse."

"You're incorrigible," she teased. "I know, I know. You warned me. Go on, say it."

"No, I understand what that lowlife wanted." He held her arms out to the sides. "Look at you. You're drop-dead gorgeous."

Cate rolled her eyes and groaned, "Please!"

Swiftly, she rose, going into the bedroom out of his sight, although she didn't shut the door. He could hear her opening drawers and the closet door.

"I'm giving up on dating," she yelled. "It's completely useless and ultimately unfulfilling. Not worth the headache." Cate strolled out dressed in her shorts and a concert tee-shirt.

"Loverboy?" he winged. Then again, he thought she was as ravishing wearing the oversized tee-shirt as she had been with a chic black dress.

"Don't worry, you have many years of dating in your future."

She put her hands on her hips. "Well, that's not encouraging. Maybe I should become a nun."

"You already are," he laughed.

"Funny," she mocked.

He pointed at her tee-shirt. "You've been to a slew of concerts, haven't you?"

"Not lately."

Kyle kicked back on the sofa, putting his socked feet up. "How's Ed doing?"

"Being a new daddy's exciting. Emily's really cute. And Ed made partner, the youngest ever in the firm's history. He must be making a boatload of change because he finally paid back the ten thousand dollars I lent him two years ago for his wedding."

"He's happy?"

"I don't know," she sighed.

"Did I ever tell you your brother threatened me?"

"He did?" Getting water from the refrigerator, she sat beside him again.

"At the concert when you ran to the restroom." He cupped his arms behind his neck. "Funny, he didn't say a word to Joseph."

"What was it?" she asked keenly.

"Not much. I got the message, though." Absentmindedly, he rubbed her cheek with the back of his hand. "You're exceptional and, therefore, untouchable. He ordered me to keep my hands off you. It was part of his 'big brother code' to kick the crap out of me if I hurt you."

She burst out laughing.

"It's not funny," he grimaced.

"Yes, it is."

"Cate, back to this Alex guy. I must have seemed crazy to you. I just had this gut instinct." He reached for her hand. "So, you're okay?"

"Yeah," she chirped.

"Cate, not every guy sees you as a piece of meat."

"Friends don't count," she giggled, brushing back his hair with a bouncy flair. Fleetingly, their gaze locked, his intense blue eyes reeling her in, their lips a whisper away from touching. Cate broke the connection and kissed his cheek. Grasping her hand when she rose, Kyle's look was filled with such a hunger that it overwhelmed her.

"Can I get you anything," her breath heavy in her chest, "before I go to bed?"

He said nothing. The room was filled with unspoken desire and unbearable muteness.

"Good night then." She flashed a doleful smile and closed the bedroom door. He shut his eyes and slid lower on the sofa, his head tilted back. *Damn*, he thought, angry at himself, drumming his fingers beside his legs while lying on the sofa.

It would be a long night.

A loud knocking at the door jarred Kyle from a deep sleep. He peered at the closed bedroom door and slowly rose from the sofa, feeling groggy yet infinitely better than two days ago. When he reached to unlatch the lock, the person outside knocked again, more aggressively.

"Okay! Hold on," grumbled Kyle loudly.

Opening the door, he was surprised to see Alex with flowers in one hand and a bottle of California sparkling wine in the other. Alex was equally stunned.

"Wow. Alex Miller," he said contemptuously.

"Yes, is Catherine here?"

"She's still in bed."

Of course, Kyle knew she was likely awake and fully dressed for her audition, but he relished each misunderstood impression Alex received from his being there.

He thought he'd rub it in a bit more. "Catie honey, there's someone here to see you."

Cate stepped out of the bedroom. "Did you say something, Kyle? Listen, I called the studio to reschedule your fitting today to Wednesday. Gives you a couple of days to …" She halted, shocked, spotting Alex standing outside the entrance and Kyle chilling against the open door with a smug expression on his face.

"Alex, hi, what a surprise! I'm just leaving for my audition." She approached the doorway, seeing the gifts Alex had brought. "Are these for me?"

Flustered, she accepted the presents from him with an awkward smile. "Thank you so much."

"Here, allow me," Kyle said as he relieved her of the gifts, lifting the flowers. "I'll put them in water. Upper cabinet for the vase, right babe?"

"Under the kitchen sink." She gave him a narrowed look.

He then held up the bottle and sneered, "And I'll put this in the fridge next to the Dom Pérignon I bought you."

She shook her head dismissively, crossing the threshold.

"Oh, sweetheart," he added with an enhanced grin, "when will you get home?" He was clearly overacting.

"Later." She squinted her eyes at him angrily.

"Catherine," interrupted Alex. "May I walk you to your car?"

"Sure," she replied timidly.

"Good luck today, sweetie," called Kyle as they left, using the flowers to wave goodbye. Cate stared back with a fiery glare. Alex also stole a glimpse back, Kyle openly scowling at him.

Closing the door, Kyle gloated under his breath, "Asshole."

***

Flinging open the apartment door, Cate entered like a whirlwind, startling Kyle, who had been napping on the sofa.

"Audition not go well?" He rubbed his face.

"No, the audition was fine. I was able to channel my frustration into my reading. They loved me! I probably got the part!" Her anger was right at the surface.

"So, you're upset because you were cast?"

"No, none of this is the audition. It's you," she fumed.

"What?" He looked at the sofa. "I've been lying here recovering from the flu."

She noticed her Bon Jovi tee-shirt. "What're you wearing?"

"I took a shower. I'm out of clean shirts and borrowed yours. You don't mind, do you?"

She looked fiercely at him. "I wore that yesterday."

He clutched the front of the shirt and brought it up to his nose. "It smells like you, like your perfume." He peeked at her adoringly. It made her melt. Remembering her displeasure with him, she jangled her senses.

"You can go home. You don't have to stay anymore," she said

snootily. "And you can wear your own clothes."

"Cate, what's wrong?" An impression of humility sprang from him.

"I'm mad at you. What was that earlier? I'm not a tree a dog marks!"

"I was merely having some fun," he chuckled. "The look on his face …"

"We had lunch after my audition, and I spent nearly the whole meal justifying us." She pointed fervently between them. "He doesn't believe nothing's going on here."

"Well, it's because he doesn't know you. But I know you, and I'd never suspect anything's happening. Besides, Cate, it's a bad sign."

"What is?"

He went to her, reached for her hand, and guided her to the sofa to sit beside him.

"That he doesn't trust you. Obviously, he doesn't have a platonic relationship with a woman. Therefore, he doesn't believe you. This is a valuable lesson." Kyle smiled to himself over the wise insight he was about to impart. "People see the world through the lens of who they are. In other words, if someone's a good liar, he's under the impression everyone lies. If he can get away with it, so can others. You, my sweet angel, are good, kind, and loving, and your lens views the world equally good, kind, and loving, which it's not. Evil's out there." He flipped back her hair from her shoulders. "If he assumes we're together, then, I give you odds, he's a womanizer."

"Not just that we're together. He thinks we're …"

"Having sex. That's what I meant by together. Anyway, he has no scruples."

"No, you're wrong. Alex is nice. Last night, he told me he'd like me to meet his parents."

"He played the *parent card*? He's definitely trying to get in your pants."

"Kyle!" she ranted. "That's a horrible thing to say."

"It's true. No guy wants a girl to meet his parents this soon."

"I met Nana after knowing you for two weeks."

"Completely different," he swore. "I wasn't conning you to get you into bed." Part of him knew that wasn't true.

"Whatever. I apparently didn't convince him we're only friends."

"If he believes we're together in any way, and he's still making a play for you, then run the other direction," he advised, fondling her fingers. "He's making moves on someone who's already taken. He has no morals."

"Huh? You've lost me."

The word hit Kyle hard. "Don't ever say that."

"What?"

Clasping her hand, he said, flustered, "That I've lost you! I don't ever wanna lose you."

"No, it's an expression. It means I don't understand."

"I know what it means. Please don't ever say it again." He swept the hair behind her ears.

"All right." She was still perplexed.

Kyle glanced at her with a puppy-dog sulk. "Are you really sending me packing?"

"No."

Cate laid her hand across his forehead. He had no fever. It was simply an excuse to touch him. "You need more soup."

Chapter 31
What Haunts in the Night

In Cate's dream ...

Kyle was holding her hand ... They seemed to be at a carnival ... In a funhouse ... She stopped, staring into a strangely distorted mirror ... At first, she was funny-looking, weird, horribly misshapen ...

Something was wrong ... She tried to pull away ... Yet she was surrounded by mirrors, all reflecting the grotesque ...

She reached for Kyle, but he was gone ...

It was past 1:30 in the morning when Kyle was abruptly awakened. Startled! It was a voice loudly wailing. "Where are you?!"

What did he hear? Shaking himself to reality, he battled to listen.

"Kyle!" Cate's voice frantically cried.

He jumped up and opened her bedroom door. She was asleep, writhing, the covers tangled tightly, strangling her legs.

"Don't leave me!" she gasped, uncontrollably shaking.

He sat on the side of her bed and gently touched her. "Catie, sweetheart, wake up. You're having a nightmare."

She wrenched herself from the grips of the ominous phantom in her subconscious. Her eyes were full of tears, sweat beading on her forehead, and labored breathing. When she realized she was in her own bed, with Kyle affectionately looking down at her, she exhaled forcefully and put her hand over her forehead, hiding beneath it.

"I'm sorry," she cried.

"No reason to be." He wiped away her tears. "I thought the nightmares had stopped after you saw the therapist the clinic recommended."

"This was different."

"How so?" He touched her face.

"It wasn't about what happened."

"Well, good, right?"

Rolling away from him, she mumbled, "No. It was worse."

"What do you mean?"

"It was so real. We were in a funhouse, like at a fair."

"We?" he asked, surprised.

"Yes, you and me. So strange! Warped mirrors and fake people jumping out from nowhere. It was frightening. And then you were gone. I couldn't find you anywhere ... and I was surrounded by crazy noises and shapes and reflections. I was lost and scared. There was no way out."

He rubbed her back, comforting her. "It would never happen. I'd never leave you alone."

Kyle straightened her blanket and laid on top of the covers next to her, putting his arm under her head. She slid up against him.

"I wanna run away from this town," she moaned.

"What? You can't go now. You're doing so well. You're making a name for yourself."

"The movie star says I'm doing well?"

Turning on his side to face her, he stroked her head. "You are. You get cast in nearly everything you're sent out on. That's unheard of. You're unbelievably talented. You can't walk away from that." He laid back. "Anyway, you can't go. What would I

Slating Magic Hour

do without you?"

"You're never even here," she huffed. "I've barely seen you this year. You wouldn't even realize I was gone."

"Yes, of course I would." Kyle sat up brusquely. "You can't go."

She rocked to her side to see him. "Don't misunderstand, please. I'm sincerely proud of you, but you have your nonstop schedule. Busy with your career and your *other* friends."

He knew what she meant.

"I miss you," she added in a forlorn voice.

"Catie, if you ever need me, I'll be here, I promise. So, stop saying you're leaving me."

"I'm not leaving *you*," she said benignly. "I wanna escape from L.A.; I mean, every audition I go to, my heart's in my throat. It haunts me."

What could he say? Nestling her close, he kissed her head.

Cate was silent for several minutes.

"Kyle, can I ask you something?"

"Sure."

Carefully, she addressed her inquiry. "Remember when you returned from location that Thanksgiving and asked me to go back with you to Seattle?"

"Yes."

"You seemed intent on getting me there." Her vision searched his face. "Did you know?"

"I had a strong suspicion," he admitted. "I saw the bruising. I put it together with your talk with Nana."

"You didn't ask." She sighed woefully.

"No. I wanted to." He weighed his words. "I was afraid I was right and didn't wanna be. Would you've told me if I had?"

"I don't know." She hid her aching. "Yes, I would've. I told Nana because I needed a mother. I couldn't tell my mom. She would've made me come home."

Deliberating how to phrase a question that had perplexed her for over two years, she finally asked, "So why fly me to Seattle?"

"To keep you from harm." His look was never more generous. "I figured no one could hurt you if you were with me. I'd watch over you. And if I did, maybe it would erase the past."

She was sullen. "I should've accepted your invitation."

"I wish I had insisted you return with me," he said urgently. "No excuses. There's no way I would've let you stay here alone if I'd known."

As he lovingly squeezed her hand, she relaxed.

"The clinic told me to call my family or a friend. I couldn't, but if they'd required it, I trusted only you." Her eyes pleaded with him, and then she shook her head. "Stupid, 'cause you were in Seattle. Far away. What could you do?"

He looked at her, astounded. "I would've jumped on the first flight back to be with you."

"Kyle, you were in the middle of filming," she reminded.

"So? I'd tell them there was a family emergency and I needed a few days off. They would've shot around me. It happens all the time on location filming."

"You'd drop everything?"

"To be with you—yes, of course!"

There was silence as she took in his warm revelation. Julia's speech pierced her mind—*He would never interrupt his career for anyone.* And yet she trusted his word was true—for her, he would have.

"The truth …" She hesitated. "I was afraid if you knew I'd always be that girl who was raped. I wouldn't be Cate to you anymore."

He tipped her head to meet her eyes. "Catie, how can you ever think that? I love …" he halted his words, caressing her head. "You're my best friend. I'll always care for you. Nothing'll ever change that."

So close to the declaration she longed to hear and yet miles away. Her mind was spinning, again devastated by a wave of sadness. The grief lingered.

"It's okay," she said bravely. "I survived on my own, and I'm stronger for it."

"The thing is, you didn't have to." He lifted her chin to meet his eyes. "And you're not that girl."

She looked devotedly at him. "You're here now."

"Try to sleep, Catie. I won't leave. Everything will be okay."

He shifted his position on the bed and adjusted the pillow. Once he was situated, he held her tighter, kissed her on the head, and shut his eyes to rest. Cate was also drifting off to sleep, cuddling against him, his arms wrapped around her, feeling secure.

Lord, Kyle thought, *she feels so good. What am I doing?*

In dawn's light, she lazily awoke to see Kyle, wide awake, lying beside her with just the sheet covering him. His shirt was off, so he must have gotten hot while he slept, she reasoned. His smile was subtle but endearing.

"Morning," he whispered. "Did you sleep well?"

"Yes. Thank you for keeping away the nightmares."

He smiled again and fondled her head, his eyes entrancing her. It made her feel odd, both anxious and excited to be near him.

"Did you sleep okay?" she asked, almost childlike.

"Honestly, no, not really. I watched you sleep instead. You seemed so peaceful," he replied affectionately.

"Oh, sorry," she blushed and didn't know why.

"No, Catie, I couldn't rest because I want ... you're so beautiful, but off limits." He shook his head. "I shouldn't say any of this. Besides, you may not feel the same way."

"No, I ..."

He embraced her. "Catie, I want you. I always have. I love you deeply."

A flush of excitement spread through her being. Gently, he held her face, bringing her near, their eyes locked, energy bursting with desire. His lips ignited her very soul.

"Oh, Kyle." She was euphoric, her body at one with his.

※

Something jolted her awake in the dark room, dawn still hours away. Kyle sat up, staring at her. He was wearing his shirt.

"Cate, you okay?"

"Yes. Why?" She needed to return to the dream.

"Catie, you were sliding so close you nearly pushed me off the bed. Another bad dream?"

"No," she breathed out, frustrated. "A really good one."

Chapter 32
Hold the Line

A hectic year later, 1993 brought a powerful script that had the industry buzzing.

Wonderwall was a classic suspense thriller about a team pulling off an impossible heist. The group consisted of two men and one woman, friends since childhood. A close acquaintance of Kyle's, Davis Whitman, wrote the screenplay. Kyle immediately approached his manager.

"Tom, this script was also written with Cate and Joseph in mind. Davis told me he patterned their characters after watching the three of us. You have to get the producers to at least interview them. They need to be given an opportunity."

Kyle's star power provided him with a tremendous negotiating advantage. Fortunately, there was no Renny to undermine him. His requests were taken seriously.

Joseph and Cate's excellent resumes and past performances persuaded the producers to cast both of them. However, they were obligated to cast a name actress as the lead character's girlfriend, a small but critical role. Bess Allen, a major rising star on Kyle's level, came on board.

※

On the weekends, the cast and crew would run over to a trendy restaurant with a karaoke bar. It was situated on a mountain overlooking the Phoenix skyline.

As they finished their dinner, energetic future-speak filling the air, Cate was lost in worries. Kyle studied her appearance. "Something bothering you, Cate?"

"It's Monday's scene," she swallowed her words.

"Why are you thinking about Monday? It's Saturday. Live in the now," jested Joseph, sitting beside his girlfriend, Jessica, who worked as a makeup artist on the production.

"Cate, what is it?" asked Kyle.

She flushed profoundly. "The scene in Langston's office."

His forehead creased, staring at her. "The kiss?"

"It's not a kiss." She inflated opening her eyes wide. "It's a *kiss*!"

"So?"

Everyone at the table stared at her, entertained. She buried her distress in drinking her ginger ale. "Never mind."

"Cate, it's a silly kiss," said Joseph. "You've done much more grueling stunts than that."

"Wait," probed Jessica. "You've kissed a guy before?"

"Sure, of course. I suppose," Cate snapped. "A peck at the end of an evening. Nothing more serious than that."

They all gawked at her.

"Well, nothing like the movies," she cringed, "where there's lots of kissing before a steamy love scene."

"The movies?" Joseph heckled. "That's your measure?!"

Jessica pursued, somewhat bemused. "Seriously, you've never made out with a guy?"

"Will you all stop looking at me like I'm a freak? I went out in groups with my pals in high school. I went out with friends, not boyfriends. I didn't go out on dates." She scooted her chair. "Just drop it."

Taken aback, Joseph and his girlfriend glanced at each other, squelching their laughter. He spotted Kyle's scolding look.

"Hey, let's lighten the mood," Joseph advanced. "Cate, why don't you try singing tonight?"

"What?" She was aghast. "No, I'll be a laughingstock. I can't even squeak out a note."

"Maybe you'd be more comfortable, Cate, if someone went up and sang with you ... Kyle?"

"Thanks, Joseph," Kyle groused. "No, sorry. It's not a good plan."

"Why? It's brilliant!" Cate came alive with the proposal.

"Because Kyle's afraid to sing in public, too," pestered Joseph. "Right, buddy?"

"No, *buddy*. I'm not afraid. I'm sensible. I'd prefer my off-key version of *Stairway to Heaven* not be broadcast on *Entertainment Tonight*."

"Kyle, how arrogant of you," he teased, looking around the room. "I don't see any cameras."

"I love to sing, Cate," volunteered Jessica. "We can do a duet."

Begrudgingly, Cate made her way to the stage beside Jessica. Flipping through the music catalog, they chose Belinda Carlisle's *Heaven is a Place on Earth*. Holding the microphone, Cate detected how clammy her palms were, her heart pounding furiously in her chest. Jessica had to begin singing first, rousing her. After a few seconds in the spotlight with her new acquaintance, Cate built up the pluck to sing fully and realized she was having fun, aglow with joy.

Kyle remembered when he first met Cate four years before. She was no longer eighteen, yet retained her youthful fire and was more comfortable on stage than he'd ever imagined. Her presence still staggered him.

After Cate returned to her seat, Kyle watched her confidence again subside, dampening her enthusiasm for the triumphant performance.

A half-hour later, Cate was the first to retreat from the restaurant. Her excuse was to study Monday's sides, but in fact, she wanted to avoid further inquiries into her naïveté.

Plagued by visions of everyone laughing at her, she had no clue how she would pull off the kissing scene. Looking back, she regretted her shyness and constant refusal to date. Where was Alex now that she needed someone to woo her? She prayed the director would give her insight to be believable.

Groaning and disillusioned, she laid back on the bed ... such a preposterous scene. Davis had found it humorous when he wrote it. Cate didn't find it the least bit funny.

The setup—Playing the role of Stevie, her mission was to distract the nemesis Langston, played by actor Eddie Tippler, with her sexy ingenuity.

Seductive skills? This can't be happening!

There was a knock at her hotel room door, startling her. She glanced at the clock on the nightstand, which read 11:30 p.m. Relatively late, she figured. Dressed in The Cars' concert tee-shirt and her underwear, she snapped up her gym shorts and slipped them on. "Who is it?"

"Cate, it's Kyle. I know it's late. May I please come in?" he said in a clandestine tone. She discreetly opened the door and let him in.

"I wanna apologize for our gang tonight. Not very sensitive of a friend. I can see you're really troubled by the scene." He inspected the room. "Cate, this place *is* small."

"Don't be envious, big guy," she joked, sitting on the corner of the bed. "It's the perks of being a supporting character."

Undecided on how to commence his mission, Kyle stared at her, sitting across from her on the side chair.

She hung her head. "All it says is *Stevie aggressively kisses Langston to distract him.* That's a vague direction. And Kyle, I've no lines. You guys are the only ones with lines."

"Ian's the type of director who'll give you the freedom to

improvise. And if you judge something needs to be said, say it. If it doesn't fit or he doesn't like it, he'll have you do it again."

"Oh, great," she surly replied. "That's not something I wanna hear."

"Cate, it's okay," he reassured, "not a big deal."

"It is to me."

"Sorry, of course." He squeezed her hand caringly. "Catie, you've always been ready and willing to help me, taking care of me when I'm sick, running lines with me." He rose before her and backed up a few feet. "The least I can do is help you with the scene."

"Huh?" She looked up, nonplused. "What do you mean?"

He motioned to her. "Stand up."

Cautiously, she stood but did not move, concern washing over her.

"I'm not gonna bite!" He grinned at her foot-dragging. "Come here," he summoned, taking her hand. "Relax. Close your eyes."

She stared at him.

"Trust me, please."

Hesitantly, she closed her eyes and sighed. Recognizing her precious vulnerability, Kyle gently kissed her.

She leaned in, and he held her close. The light kiss became more tenderly urgent, lasting over a few moments. When he stopped, pulling away just enough to part their lips, she faltered, dizzy with stirrings. She opened her eyes to see his dashing face, her heart pounding excitedly.

"That was really nice. Is that all there is to it?" she asked, relieved.

"No, there's more."

Drawing her into an impassioned embrace, he pressed his mouth to hers, tasting her breath as he shared his. It lasted for quite a while. He needed to curb himself, engaging the acting coach he was attempting to be. Cate, alive with the heat of the moment, clung to him as he slowly ended the kiss.

Her look begged him, full of longing, breathless. "Did I ... did I do okay?"

"Yeah." He paused, lost in the flush of pleasure, trying to fix again on the task. "Very good. Yes, you're a quick study. That's what the director expects to see."

"You're a good instructor," she smiled demurely.

"Just being a friend. Did you get a feel for it?"

"I felt it everywhere," she said, still gasping with desire.

"Right." It was definitely time to leave.

He walked to the door. "Hope that helps."

"Wait! Shouldn't I practice being the one who, ya know, starts the kiss? It's in the script."

Kyle doubted his limits. Did he dare to hold her again?

"I think you'll be fine."

"The scene'd be so much easier if you were the one I was kissing," she said breathlessly.

"Goodnight, Cate." He flashed a brief smile and exited.

Once outside, he reclined against her door, exhausted, trying to clear the arousal.

⁂

Cate stepped onto the set, costumed in form-fitting leather jeans, a tight button blouse, and high-heeled pumps. Ian Parrish told her to hit her mark but feel free to "play with the scene." Adjusting her collar, she noticed the camera angle and devised a strategy.

⁂

SCENE: Standing in the background, Mike Langston—late thirties, athletic, and attractive—is in a heated phone conversation, toying with the card access key they need to pilfer.

The camera is close on three characters—Stevie (Cate), Eric (Joseph), and Charlie (Kyle). Eric and Charlie are standing at the far exit of the spacious office, secretly plotting their mission to make the casual switch. Stevie is behind them, swaying to the beat of an alternative rock station playing *Radioactive* by The Firm. With saucy confidence, she undoes two buttons of her blouse. Cleavage exposed, she adjusts her tight leather jeans. She yanks off the rubber band holding her ponytail, and shakes her long, flowing hair.

"Action ..."

Stevie strides between Eric and Charlie, shoving them apart, and moves seductively to Langston.

Langston's eyes bulge at her sexiness, blatantly looking her up and down. "Hey, I'll call you back." He abruptly hangs up the phone.

Leaning against his desk, Langston shoots a quick stare at Charlie for his reaction before returning his attention to Stevie.

"Wyler's little sister, the charming and talented Stevie, all grown up," he leers. "Did you come here looking for a job?"

"Not really. It's just that powerful men make me hot."

Without hesitation, she grabs him by the jacket lapels and propels him into his chair. She snatches the coveted access card from his hand and tosses it on the desk, freeing his hands to place them on her backside, swiveling the chair, his back to the guys. Stevie straddles Langston in the chair and kisses him passionately, running one hand through his hair. She places the other hand on the top of the chair and gestures at the access device while continuing the vigorous kissing.

Eric rushes over, snatches the keycard from the desk, and makes the switch before he and Charlie inch toward the exit, totally shocked by what they are witnessing.

Charlie clears his throat and calls, "I hate to interrupt, Stevie, but we need to go."

Sharply, Stevie breaks the clinch. She scoffs at them indignantly and stands up to straighten herself.

"Wait a minute!" Langston catches her arm.

"Later, cowboy, I'm late for work." She playfully touches his nose with the tip of her finger. "Maybe another time …"

Parading to Eric and Charlie, she notices their stunned expressions. She says in a low voice, "What? Did you just notice I'm a girl?!"

"And cut."

"That was great, Cate. Good reactions, everyone," said Ian with an approving laugh, Davis pulling him aside.

"Ian, this gives me an idea for the end of the story," Davis said eagerly. "Just a slight tweak."

As Kyle stared at Cate, speechless, Joseph leaned in and nudged him.

"I guess watching movies can be educational after all."

Chapter 33
Vista

The magestic vista seemed to breathe life into the rugged mountain range, a short drive from the resort where the cast was housed for the shoot. It had a family-friendly park atmosphere with a choice of intrepid and direct trails to the top of the mountain.

"Thanks for coming along on the walk today," said Cate. "The local crew keeps telling me it's a great hike. An easy climb. We can do it in an hour if we hustle."

"Hustle?" Joseph groaned. "I'm up for a leisurely stroll. It's hot in these jeans."

"Sorry, Joseph, this is Phoenix in the summertime. People don't wear jeans." She rubbed his arm sympathetically. "So, how come I lucked out and got you all to myself for a change? Where's Jessica today?"

"She's working. She has to work even when we aren't."

Handing him one of the bottles of water she was carrying, she noted, "I've never seen you this dedicated to being with a girlfriend. Even with Lilly."

"It's nice. Jessica's in the business, and she gets it. And I won't get dumped like Lilly did to me."

"Well, I'm pleased for you and Jessica."

He began to slightly pant. "Cate, you told me this trek up the damn mountain would be easy."

"It's good exercise."

"Speaking of exercise, when will you begin dating? In all the years I've known you, I've never heard you say you went out on a date."

"Last year with Alex. You know, the guy I brought to the wedding. But it didn't go too well." She looked away and added, "Besides, Kyle did everything in his power to ensure nothing went on between Alex and me."

Joseph's ears perked up, and he stared at Cate, speechless, his mind sifting through this new information. "When it comes to you, Kyle's messed up."

"What do you mean?" she curiously muttered.

"Kyle ..." He sought to find the words. "He worries about you. We all do."

Not what she hoped; she shook her head. "Geez. I'm a big girl. I can take care of myself."

"So, one date *last* year?"

"I'm too busy now," she said briefly, ending the topic.

They came to a viewing area.

Taking a big gulp from the bottled water, he scoffed, "No one's that busy."

Cate rapidly exclaimed, "Oh, what a view! Spectacular, isn't it?"

"Yes, it is." He stiffly stared out over the landscape.

The sun drenched her face with resplendent light as she experienced its magnificence. "Worth the hike?"

"Sort of." Peering carefully over the ledge, he became pale and dizzy. "Can we get off this mountain now?"

"Sure."

They traversed down the trail at a fairly quick pace. Too fast. Joseph slipped. Cate gripped his arm to keep him from falling.

"Joseph, whoa, slow down. What's wrong?"

"Did I ever tell you I don't care for high places?"

"You're afraid of heights?"

"Petrified."

He bent over, taking calming breaths with his hands on his knees.

She anxiously leaned down to make eye contact. "Joseph, why didn't you tell me? I wouldn't have asked you to do this with me."

"No, it's been a while since we've hung out." He concentrated on his breathing.

"Next time, we'll hang out at the pool," she said.

"Definitely."

At the trail's end, they came to the picnic area overlooking the city. A family was having a birthday party at one of the tables. Under the care of their doting parents, children laughed joyfully, running all over the place, fueled by overindulgent cake and sodas.

In the parking lot, Joseph waited as Cate dragged a tabloid paper from her car. "Have you seen this?" Her face seemed to glimmer. "It's the three of us. On the front page!"

He took the paper and read the caption: *Kyle Weston & Friends.* "Cool! We're *friends*," he jeered.

She snatched it back, putting it in the car. "Hey, at least they think we're important enough to feature on the front page."

"Cate, it's Kyle they wanted. We're like background extras."

"Well, I think it's exciting."

Joseph checked his wristwatch. "Wanna get back to the resort? I'm supposed to have dinner with Jessica."

"No, you go. I'm staying here for a while. The sun's setting. Thanks for spending the afternoon with me."

"This was fun," he said, heading to his car.

She gave him an incredulous look.

"Okay," he confessed. "Being with you was fun. The top of the mountain part—not so much."

Sitting on top of the picnic table, Cate reclined, propped up with her arms, the sun baking its heat upon her. She turned on the portable CD player hooked to her belt and pulled out her headphones. Staring out beyond the horizon, she intently listened to *Alone* by Heart.

'Til now, I always got by on my own.

The words spoke to a limitless yearning. It was her choice to be alone. She had never had a real boyfriend, no relationships, nor did she miss what she hadn't experienced. As she saw it, her life was full of love from family and loyal friends. Her career was going strong and on an upward trend. What more did she need? It was fine to be solitary with her dreams, her longings, her secrets.

I never really cared until I met you.

Kyle. Her best and most challenging relationship. So complicated. To lose him would destroy her. He meant so much to her, yet he only held her as a friend ... a kid at that.

Joseph gave the valet the keys to his rental car and strode through the resort lobby. Kyle had arrived earlier from filming, showered, and changed. He walked toward the dining room, catching sight of his friend.

"Hey Joseph," he yelled. "I called your room."

"Hi, Kyle. Done for the day?" They met near the middle of the lobby.

"Yeah, it was a good day. What did you do?"

"Cate and I hiked the mountain. Invigorating exercise to the top."

"I thought you were afraid of heights."

"I am," said Joseph. "I hated to burst her bubble. She wanted to see the view."

Indicating the restaurant off the lobby, Kyle asked, "Have you had dinner yet? I'm getting ready …"

"Oh, sorry, Kyle. I'm meeting Jessica for dinner at this fantastic Mexican restaurant." He slipped a piece of paper to him. "You're welcome to come along."

"Thanks anyway. I'll leave you two love birds to your own devices. I'll see if Cate's hungry. Is she in her room?"

"No, I left her at that little park at the base of the hike. She's watching the sunset."

"You left her at the park by herself?!"

"Yeah, why not?" Joseph looked stumped. "She had her car, and there were families with children there with her. She's fine."

"Damn it!" Charging to the valet station, Kyle snatched his keys for his rental and jumped into the vehicle.

Joseph watched the car tear away.

The glow of the sky was crimson, golden, and orange when the sun touched the horizon. It radiated a soothing gleam, hypnotizing Cate as she stared into the heavens. She was pleasantly surprised to see Kyle jogging toward her.

"Well, hello, this is a treat." Her eyes shined.

"I heard this is *the* place to watch the sunset."

She nodded, her smile growing, coaxing him to sit with her.

He took a seat on top of the picnic table beside her.

"How did you …"

"I bumped into Joseph, and he told me about your adventure." He scanned the area, which was deserted. "You know, Cate, you shouldn't be alone out here."

"Shhh …" Her vision stayed on the sunset. "Look. It's magic hour."

Kyle followed her eyes to the horizon, the sun dipping below it, leaving a kiss of color and light behind. Beautiful, serene, shimmering with hope. Enough illumination to see the world at its most unspoiled moment.

He gazed at her. In the brilliance of the setting sun, she was breathtaking. Again, the realization … always a breath away from capturing her in a hungry embrace.

The summer heat was unyielding. Even the fickle breeze did not cool. It merely moved the suffocating air. And yet, Cate relished the experience. Her thoughts drifted to memories of Kyle's kindness—how he could make her feel whole and peaceful. A rush of affection caused her to grapple with her need to be loved by him, a recurring dream of tenderness and ardor.

After several minutes of quiet, listening to the cicadas, she turned to him.

"Did you come for the view or to ensure I was safe?"

A bloom of love arrested his mood. He clashed with the impulse to kiss her. "Both. But, truly, it freaked me out that you were alone in the dark in a public park."

"I'm glad you came here so I could share this with you." Her words floated to him like a melody. Kyle realized she had become the music of his life.

"Time to get back." She stood up, brushed off her shorts, and hopped into her car to start it.

He didn't move.

"Aren't you coming?"

Hiking to her car, he bent forward into the open driver's window, Cate turning down REO Speedwagon's *Keep Pushin's* volume.

"Cate, I …" He stopped.

The tune had wrecked his courage. "This song … your best recollection?"

He silently berated himself. Why didn't he have the guts to tell her?

"Well, I can imagine yours," she jibed, then looked at him wisely. "For me, it's kind of my life story. No matter what hand I'm dealt, I keep pushin' on."

"Yeah, you do, Miss Resilience," he said admiringly. "Wanna get a bite to eat?"

"Sure, thanks."

"Joseph told me about this great Mexican restaurant." He pulled out the slip of paper from his front pocket to show her. "We could try it."

"Yeah."

"Okay." He tapped her window ledge. "Follow me."

"Always," she vowed fondly under her breath.

The stars began to appear in the darkened sky.

Chapter 34
The Casita

With a two-day break ahead for the weekend, they were hanging out in Kyle's casita. It had been a hard work week with exceedingly long hours drawing on endless light rays. It was also a physical film. There were lots of chases and, to Joseph's dismay, climbing out on bridges. Of course, their stunt doubles did the heavy lifting, yet they would do it themselves if an activity or stunt were not deemed dangerous. Cate was exhausted.

***

Dressed in jean shorts and an oversized Foreigner concert tee-shirt, knotted on the side so it wouldn't be baggy, Cate tried to locate a comfy spot on the odd-shaped loveseat with a center drink console. No matter her position, the console was in the way, making it cumbersome. She kept squirming around to find a better spot.

Kyle was reading his script in a cushioned recliner, and Joseph sat in a sizable chair beside him, channel surfing.

Peering over his script, he grinned. "What's going on over there, Catie?"

"Kyle, this is the most uncomfortable couch I've ever sat on."

Never taking his sight off the TV, Joseph gave her a heads-up. "That's because it's not a couch. It's a double recliner."

"Not conducive to a good nap," she trifled, hanging her legs over the center bump.

"Well," Kyle suggested humorously, "you can always rest in your huge room."

"And deprive you of my company? Never," she quipped.

"Well, I'm out of here," Joseph announced. "Jessica's meeting me for dinner." He stood up and handed her the remote.

"Joseph, you're the luckiest man, Jessica getting a makeup artist job on the same production." She aimed the remote and turned off the TV. "How often does that happen?"

"More often than you'd expect," said Kyle, turning the page. "The industry's a small community."

"Until tomorrow." Joseph crossed to the door and opened it. "Have a nice night."

"Hey, Joseph?" She had a naughty twinkle in her eye.

"Yes, Cate."

To keep from giggling, she bit her lower lip. "Need any condoms?"

Joseph squinted, annoyed. "This role's made you way too sassy."

"I've always had gumption. You guys never paid attention."

Exaggerating his goodbye, he bowed. "Good night, Ms. Leigh."

"Good night, Mr. Beason," she said freshly.

Laughing, Joseph stepped out, closing the door behind him.

Kyle sat amused, shaking his head while underlining his script.

Exploring the refrigerator, Cate rooted around the freezer section. Standing in the center of the room, she had difficulty getting a fork into a large slice of frozen carrot cake.

"Kyle, why did you freeze this?" she grunted. "I can't cut it."

"It was melting on the counter," he answered, setting down his script.

"Well, there's an 'in-between' level called a refrigerator."

Spying her many failed attempts to stab the cake, he broke

into a smile. "Catie, come here."

She stopped in front of him. He took the plate from her, picked up the frozen cake in his hand, and held it out.

"What?" She backed away, tapering her look at him.

Extending the cake, he insisted, "Take a bite."

She took a nibble, sitting on the arm of the chair. He had one, too.

"What would you like to do for dinner?" he mumbled, his mouth full. "We can't live on carrot cake."

"No big date tonight?"

"Nope." Handing her the plate, he licked his fingers. "Leave this out for a few minutes, and it'll thaw."

She placed the plate on the side table, crossing her arms and smiling. "No available babes?"

"Plenty of offers. Not interested."

"Really? Give your pal the last of the condoms?"

"You make me sound easy."

"If the shoe fits, Cinderella."

"Ya know, Joseph's right. Playing Stevie is making you feisty," he chuckled. "So, for dinner, where should we go?"

Pitching herself onto the clumsy loveseat, she yawned. "I'm too tired to go out to eat."

"I could call room service."

"Good idea," she said, stretching. "I'd love a salad, please."

Making a face, he apprised, "Carrot cake and a salad's not a decent meal. Have a steak."

"If you insist," she said sleepily. "Medium rare, please."

Kyle picked up the phone and made his order.

"Two rib-eyes, medium rare. Two salads." Covering the mouthpiece, he solicited, "Balsamic dressing?"

She gave a nod, fighting the need to nap.

"Yeah, house dressing. Do you have a bottle of Veuve Clicquot demi-sec … no, it has to be demi-sec … Well, bring a bottle of Dom Pérignon then."

She briskly became alert, sitting up to face him. "Champagne?"

"Yeah, I missed your birthday again," he innocently said. "I owe you a bottle."

※

It was a fine meal for room service, and Cate became aware that the alcohol did not go to her head with real food in her stomach, perking her up, no longer tired.

The conversation was engaging. They hadn't simply sat and spoken for a long while. Since the loveseat was cramped, they relaxed on the floor, sharing the rest of the carrot cake.

"It was lonely after my parents died," Kyle began. "Living with Nana ... she was wonderful ... I loved that she always attended my sports and school plays. But it was only just the two of us. I envied my friends who had siblings. Which is why I plan to have a big family if I ever get married."

"Define big." She scraped the final bit of the frosting and crumbs from the empty plate.

"Three kids. Two boys and a girl."

"Wow, you're specific," she said. "Guys are lucky. They can wait practically forever before starting a family."

"Well, I have to wait until I have a wife."

"Not in Hollywood," she said coyly.

"Cate, I'm nothing like Hollywood." Elevating the glass to eye level to drift away in the bubbles, he added, "It's not my style."

The comment dumbfounded Cate. Kyle splattered on the tabloid covers was the definition of Mr. Hollywood.

Clearing her mind of meddling notions she returned the subject to siblings. "Well, I adore having a brother. Of course, I had no choice being the second child. If you talk to Ed, he may tell you a different story. He had six years of being the only child—spoiled rotten—before I ruined his world. It's what he'd tell me when we were younger."

"Nah, your brother loves you. He wouldn't be protective if he didn't. And no matter what the excuse, he enjoys taking you to concerts and spending time with you. You have a great brother." He grabbed the champagne bottle, poured another for himself, and topped off her glass. "I guess Joseph's kind of my brother. We bicker like siblings."

"And I'm your kid sister?"

The room almost pulsated with silence as Kyle raised the glass to his lips, trapping any reaction from spilling out.

Deciding to brave the inquisitiveness inundating her mind and fueled by champagne's liquid nerve, she wondered if he would continue to be candid.

"Your girlfriends ..." she began.

Kyle nudged her playfully. "Cate, I don't have girlfriends."

She rolled her eyes.

"All right," he conceded, "Julia was a girlfriend." Bristling, he tossed his hands in the air. "I suppose Jacqueline, too. Every other woman was a fling."

"Okay," she touted, "of all the women you dated, anyone you'd marry?"

"Nope," he declared.

"Really?" She was feeling exceptionally nosey. "What if you had to pick one?"

He placed his forehead against hers. "Except, I don't."

"Play along. Of the women you've been with, who?"

With an exasperated sigh, he said, "Julia, and only because she knew me before my fame. Oh, wait. She's already married! I'm off the hook," he laughed.

"In high school, did you love her?"

"No, I liked her." He leaned close to Cate. "I find liking someone's more important than even love. It's a critical first step in any relationship."

Cate became riveted by his logic.

"I mean," he continued, "I know couples who claim they love each other but actually dislike the other person. That's empty and doomed." He rattled his head to cease being so serious. "Anyway, Julia's a friend, and I care for my friends."

Tweaking her nose, he lightened the mood. "I like you." His handsome visage had a friskiness about it.

Incessantly, she dug deeper. "So, never been in love?"

"With those women? No! It was fun, but only physical, nothing more. Don't get me wrong, I'd like to be in love with that one woman, where everything about her is beyond beautiful. Yes, that's a different story."

Kyle felt wedged, a need to escape. This was a subject he wanted to avoid, especially with Cate.

"Instead of interrogating me," he sidetracked, "let's play a new game."

For entertainment, Kyle turned on the radio to a station playing classic tunes from the fifties and sixties. They invented a competition to perform each song, taking turns singing for the other. As the bottle emptied, they resolved to show off each type of dance alphabetically—along with the hits of the past. He grabbed her hand to do a fast swing when *Rockin' Robin* by Bobby Day played, and her face lit up with elation.

The fun was just beginning.

When Bobby Darin's *Beyond the Sea* came on, Kyle pulled her into his arms. "This was Nana's favorite song," he said, singing along softly.

She giggled, "I think we were born too late."

"No, we were born exactly when we were supposed to."

"Really? You keep telling me I'm way too young."

The music changed to the Beatles' *And I Love Her*, and they flowed into a rumba.

"Not anymore, tiny dancer," he dallied.

After waltzing to *Catch the Wind* by Donovan, they did a dizzy bop to the Beach Boys' *Fun, Fun, Fun*, singing at the top of their lungs.

They laughed so hard it hurt. Cate, holding her side, collapsed on the loveseat.

He watched her again try to unearth a restful place. "Cate, you look so uncomfortable. Come with me."

Grasping her hand, he led her into the bedroom. There he grabbed a pillow and tossed it to the footboard of the four-post bed with a satin comforter.

"You sit there." He pointed to the head of the bed while he sat, facing her, where he had tossed the pillow.

"Do you remember, Kyle, when we went surfing after my brother's wedding and tried to teach Joseph how to stand on a board?"

"Yeah, I had always considered him athletic, but he was a klutz," he hooted.

"An untrainable klutz at that," she said, shaking her head.

"I also recall that day, you wore a one-piece suit, not a bikini. Why?"

"When surfing, the waves can rip off tops rather easily, silly."

"Never thought of that," he grinned.

They resumed reminiscing about the crazy antics they had shared over the years. Another hour passed. The clock struck twelve.

※

After midnight, the radio station changed its playlist to ballads and love songs.

I've been waiting for a girl like you ...

Kyle nodded at her concert tee-shirt. "Foreigner. Good show?"

She pulled the front of her shirt, loosened the knotted side, and peered down at the writing. "I wouldn't know. I never saw them perform live. Ed met Foreigner's rep at the firm one day and told him how I loved their music. He sent this to Ed to give to me. A bit too big."

"Very nice." His vision locked on her allure.

"Thank you," she blushed.

"I was talking about the song," he kidded.

"Goofball," she laughed. "It's my favorite too."

Smiling, he slid his fingers on the satin cover and tickled the bottom of her feet.

"Stop …" she laughed, pulling her legs back.

Catching the warmth of her eyes as she shyly looked at him, Kyle lingered in the moment.

I've been waiting for a girl like you …

With the music underscoring the unintentional romantic backdrop, there were no thoughts, only emotions. Cate reveled in the song, swaying to the music, eyes closed. Kyle was spellbound, not simply her beauty or her heart … it was her vibrancy. He hadn't planned any of it. He honestly hadn't. Even so, why hesitate?

Tipping forward, he placed his hands on her hips, holding onto the belt loops of her shorts, and carefully slid her toward him while moving nearer to her.

At first, she shivered, expecting him to remain playful and perhaps tickle her again. Looking into his eyes, however, she was aware of the depth of his gaze, the sensual energy emanating from him.

"Ever since we practiced that scene," he whispered. "In truth, the moment I first saw you. Cate, you're so beautiful."

His lips softly touched hers.

Cate breathed into it, surrendering to her longings—every breath as one. *Is this happening*? The yearning intensified. She reached up and caressed his head. Her response gave him the confidence to kiss her more passionately, hold her tighter and lay her back on the bed.

As he kissed her neck, his hand pushed up her shirt. Opening his eyes, he lightly touched his lips to her silky, flat stomach. He heard her deep sigh—her breathing bated, her pulse quickening.

Suddenly, he felt intruded—his mind invaded by distant bruises. *Why? That doesn't matter to me. But she was so hurt ...*

He slowly sat up, ladened, his mind pulling him away from her. Angry at himself, he scolded his inner monologue. *Stop thinking, Fool. This is Cate.*

Too late. Lost in a fog of ecstasy, Cate became startled. "What is it? Did I do something wrong?"

"No, never," he said, stroking her head.

Frightened by his abrupt restraint, she begged, "Then why?"

Why? He froze, seeking a plausible excuse. "You've never been with anyone, have you?"

Slowly turning to her side, she buried her face in the covers, which muffled her voice. "No, not of my own free will."

The statement was brutal, stabbing him in the heart. He hurt for her. Why did he say that? "That's not ..."

"I've been waiting," she said hastily.

"For what?" He gently rubbed her shoulder.

Cate rolled onto her back. His blue eyes softened her mood with affection. "For you."

"Cate, I'm ..." Kyle was ruffled, hanging back.

She panicked. "Was I terrible? You know I learn fast."

"No, you're wonderful."

Overwhelmed with frustration, she covered her face with her hands. "Kyle, do you think I'm damaged goods?"

"No! Cate, don't ever say that. That's not why." He held both of her arms to get her attention.

"So why?" She appeared shattered.

Releasing her arms, he shifted slightly away from her. "Because you're not a one-night stand."

As tears pooled in her eyes, she struggled to keep them from falling. "I never thought I was."

"You're not." His mind scattered.

No, wait, it has nothing to do with what happened to her. And it's certainly not because she's astoundingly inexperienced. No, that makes me love her more. My God! That's the reason. I love her. I truly love her.

Kyle faltered. He knew his history. Hot burning and short-lived flings, never coveting permanence.

But Cate's different. She's not like anyone else.

He craved so much more. It spooked him.

"I don't understand any of this," she sighed, pushing her hair back from her forehead.

"I'm sorry. You're incredible. Amazing." He could hear his conscience, which sounded a lot like his grandmother.

Resisting her tears, she pressed backward to the head of the bed. "I should go."

"Please stay," he pleaded with a look of devotion.

"What for?" Pain echoed in her voice.

"To be … just don't leave. Please."

Again, it was not what she wanted. Her mind screamed. *I want you to tell me you love me … you want me.* But she could not say it, feeling humiliated, her heart splintered.

Kyle clutched his pillow and crawled to the head of the bed, lying beside her. He scooped her into his arms, cuddling her tenderly.

"Cate, may I ask a favor? For now, let's just take a time out, okay?"

"Sure," she said, not understanding anything that occurred.

Kissing her forehead, he added, "And we can fall asleep this way." He shut his eyes.

She stared out into the dark blankly—confused, hurt, spent—and rested her head on his chest. She should leave, and yet …

※

A knock at the door awakened Kyle, Cate snuggling next to him. Carefully, he slid away, trying not to wake her. He shut the bedroom door, making his way to answer the knock. It was

Gavrihel

Joseph holding a fast-food bag.

"Morning. Sleeping in? Jessica's busy today, so I figured we'd get Cate and drive up north, maybe stop in Sedona. I bet she'd get a kick out of … what happened here?" Joseph eyed the room service tray with dirty dinner plates and a champagne bucket holding an empty upside-down bottle of Dom. "Did you meet someone after I left?"

"No, it's not what it looks like."

Cate awoke, realizing Kyle was gone. She climbed off the bed and yanked her unknotted tee-shirt to straighten it, completely hiding the jeans shorts she wore underneath.

She opened the door, calling Kyle's name as she entered the sitting room.

Joseph stared at her, appalled. Her hair messed up, she was wearing nothing but a tee-shirt.

"I see I'm disturbing you," he angrily said to Kyle, storming out.

Kyle turned to her. "I'll be right back."

He chased his friend down as he turned the corner near the next casita. "Joseph, wait."

Tossing the fast-food bag in the trash container he passed, Joseph tersely stopped, turning to confront him. "I suppose I should say good for you, but it's not what I feel." He raised his closed fist. "I wanna punch you in the face … hard."

"Joseph, I swear it's not how it looks. Nothing happened."

"Yeah, sure," he said sarcastically.

"No. Nothing. We fell asleep talking."

"Talking? Champagne? You're full of crap!"

"We were celebrating her birthday," Kyle hurriedly said, trying to reassure his pal. "As friends."

"I begged you to let her be, Kyle. She's the sweetest girl in the world, and you can't resist the conquest!"

"I'm in love with her." The words escaped before Kyle could stop them.

Shocked, they gaped at each other, the words echoing between them. Breaking the silence, Joseph stammered, "Love? What does it mean? How exactly does Kyle Weston define love?"

Waiting for a response, Joseph's anger heightened as his friend stared vacantly.

"Kyle, it tears her up when she sees you on the cover of a magazine with some other woman. Her heart breaks because—and this is the saddest part—she fell for you like so many others." He turned and paused. "If you think about it, if you love her and yet you're with all those other women, it's like you're cheating on her. Isn't that against your code?" He glared at Kyle with disgust. "You don't deserve her. Way too good for you. She's …" He threw up his hands and rushed off.

"Perfect," Kyle sighed.

※

Returning to the casita, Kyle mulled over everything Joseph had said. *It's not true. I'm only thinking of Cate's best interest. That's why I stopped last night.*

He would protect her from anyone who might hurt her, including himself.

※

Cate was sitting on the unwieldy loveseat when Kyle entered the casita.

"What did you say?" she asked fearfully.

"The truth. Nothing happened." Shutting the door, he remained beside it.

"Oh." She stared at the floor.

"What?"

"I thought ..."

"Nothing happened, Cate," he said sternly.

"Right. I need to go." She slowly put her sandals on and walked to the door. When she passed him, she kissed his cheek. "Thanks for a memorable belated birthday," she said quietly.

He never turned, hearing only the click of the door.

The next day on set was tough; the three stayed apart until it was necessary to shoot a scene. Cate could corral the inconvenient and inappropriate emotions she was experiencing and channel them into her performance. It amazed everyone on set, especially Kyle and Joseph. They were both unfocused.

Chapter 35
The Call

In the living room of their new home in Bel Air, Julia listened to Cate's tenuous message on the answering machine. John watched Julia impatiently pace as the hotel connected to Cate's room.

"Sweetie, it's Julia. What's wrong? You seemed upset."

"Oh, Julia." Her voice was desperate. "Thank you for calling me back. Actually, I wasn't sure who to ask because it's about Kyle."

"Kyle? What did he do?" she snarled, anger rising, her protective instinct toward Cate triggered.

"Nothing. And that's the problem."

"What do you mean?" Julia plopped down on the sofa, sitting close to her husband, who could now eavesdrop on Cate's conversation.

"We were having a nice evening together the other night, and one thing led to another …" Cate hesitated. "And then Kyle told me he needed a time-out. Julia, I don't understand. Why?"

"Let me get this straight." She shot a worried look at John. "You were about to do the deed, and Kyle stopped?! Mankind's gift to women? That Kyle? He stopped?"

"Yeah, but you were the one who told me that he was a good guy who'd never take advantage."

"I meant he wouldn't start anything. Not stop in the middle."

Cate moaned. "See why I'm so confused."

"Did he say anything?"

"He said I wasn't a one-night stand. He was very ..."

"Very what?" Julia sounded anxious.

"Kind and loving, and yet he pulled away. I started to leave, and he asked me to stay. He held me all night as we slept. Julia, I don't understand. I feel so ashamed."

"No, sweetie, don't. It wasn't you. It was him."

Cate shook her head. "I still don't get it."

"Think about it, Cate. John and I were talking about how Kyle looks at you when we're all together and how considerate he is to you. Kyle brags that he doesn't do love. Except it's so plain ... he's in love with you."

"Can't be," Cate groaned. "He acts like he only wants to be my friend. I've given him plenty of clues. Maybe I'm being naïve."

"If he didn't love you, why else would he have a conscience?!"

"Julia, I can't even ... If he only wants a friend, I guess I have to live with that. But I'm in love with *him*."

"I want to smack him upside the head." Julia turned solemn. "Here's my best advice. Do as Kyle asks and take a break. Give him some space and time. He's gonna realize ... it'll work out."

Chapter 36
Listen to Your Heart

There were only a couple of days left to film. As far as Joseph was concerned, the prickliness between them needed to end.

Cate was reviewing her script when he strolled up. "Hey, can we talk?"

She peeked up with an embarrassed light and nodded. He dragged over another chair to sit next to her as she put away her script.

"I believe it might be mature of me to talk to my dearest friend."

"Joseph." She lowered her head. "I'm sorry."

"For what?"

"The way it looked," she breathed out heavily.

"Looks can be deceiving. I know nothing took place. That's not what upset me." He moved in closer to be more private. "I was cross because I didn't want you to get hurt. And it troubles me that you can't see you're headed into a heartbreak."

"I'm not."

"Cate, your friends love you. Julia, John, me, we're trying to protect you because you don't recognize what's occurring."

She glimpsed at him, baffled. "You think I'm a kid."

"No, you're an adult," he said, "which is even more dangerous."

"Why?"

Joseph was torn. "Kyle's not into relationships. He's a love 'em and leave 'em kind of guy. You deserve far more than a fling."

She contemplated why everyone perceived Kyle as callous when time and again, he had dropped what he was doing, no matter how important, to be there for her.

"No, that's not true," she chided. Maybe he'd understand if she shared what Kyle had done to care for her. "Joseph, there's something you don't know."

"Okay," he posed, willing to listen.

Assembling her feelings, she questioned whether she should gamble sharing that tragic day. Only Kyle knew. It was her bond with him. She changed her mind.

"Nothing," she mumbled, looking away.

Stifling a laugh, he said compassionately, "Cate, it's not a big secret."

"What?" Her eyes zipped to his face. Did he already know somehow?

"That you're ..." He wrestled with the term. "Innocent."

Not what she feared at all. *Gee, Julia's right. It must be written across my forehead!*

"And it's part of the problem," he said.

"Sorry, I'd think waiting for the right man would be good."

"It is. It's unique and special," he confirmed. "Do you really believe it's Kyle?"

"Yes," she said without hesitation.

Studying her hands in her lap, she took a moment. "I love him. I always have. Joseph, I've tried to listen to your advice, but it's Kyle. You and Julia constantly tell me he's selfish and only cares about himself. Not with me. He's always been thoughtful and giving. He's seen me through some of the most difficult moments of my life. It's like you two are talking about someone else ... not Kyle." She paused. "Maybe I'm kidding myself."

Sitting back, Joseph stared at her with wonder. How could he have missed the signs? Yes, he suspected she had a crush on Kyle, but now, he clearly saw she was deeply in love.

It suddenly hit him that he had misjudged Kyle's intentions. He took her hand.

"Cate, you're right. Kyle's a good person, and I think he tries to convince himself he only cares about his career."

"Joseph, I called Julia, and she said Kyle's in love with me. That's crazy, right? I mean, something could've happened that night, but ... he didn't. I really don't think he sees me that way."

"*He* didn't?" Searching Cate's face full of love and need, Joseph finally fully understood. "The truth's obvious to everyone but Kyle, Cate. He can't express his feelings because he fears love and, at the same time, losing you."

Her disorientation heightened. "What?"

"Not many of us get to know a real live angel like you. It can be daunting." He hugged her. "Can I have my friend back?"

"I never left." She tightened the embrace.

"Ahem."

They broke their hug and turned to see Mindy, a production assistant, awkwardly trying to get Cate's attention.

"Excuse me, Ms. Leigh. I have a change of schedule for you." She presented a new call sheet and some revised script pages.

"What's this?" Cate asked curiously, Joseph hanging over her shoulder to get a look.

"This is your schedule for San Francisco next week," said Mindy. "I've already booked your air and hotel."

"What do you mean, next week? I thought we'd wrap this week in Phoenix."

Mindy pointed to a huddled group across the way in an animated conversation with Kyle. "You might ask them because I'm not sure." She walked away.

"This is your chance." Joseph nudged her. "Go talk to Kyle."

Seeing Kyle standing there, Cate's stomach turned with nerves, and she dreaded this encounter despite Joseph's urging.

"Joseph," she whined, making a pained face.

"Go," he ordered with a chuckle.

As Cate approached, the group dispersed, leaving only Kyle chatting with Davis, who waved her over.

"Hi," Cate said brightly to Davis. "What's this?"

"Cate, new sides. I made a change to the ending ... everyone loves it. So you and Kyle will shoot in San Francisco for a few days."

"Okay," she muttered slowly, feeling uneasy.

"An exciting twist to film in the city by the bay," Davis said enthusiastically. "This'll be great." He squeezed her arm and wore a huge smile, marching back to the set, leaving Cate and Kyle alone.

She tried to catch Kyle's eye as he looked away.

"Surprising," she managed to say.

"Not really. It's a better ending. We all agreed."

A disquieted stasis estranged them, the distance feeling unbearable. Cate stared down, wanting to crawl into the pages she held.

"So," he sheepishly continued, "how are you?" The tension was unyielding.

"Fine. You?" She searched his sad eyes. No matter how they tried to avoid it, their attraction still overwhelmed them.

Taking a labored breath, he began, "Cate, about the other night ..."

"Kyle, please, we don't need to talk about it."

"We do," he insisted.

"No." She steadied herself. "It's forgotten."

"It is?"

Heeding Julia's advice, Cate marshaled her will and resilience.

"Sure. That's what you want, right? That we take a step back and just be good friends."

"Cate, I ..."

Leaning forward, she kissed his cheek and gave a demure

smile. "I'm cool with that." Turning, she quickly walked to her trailer and closed the door.

Kyle sat alone at the table eating his dinner, a half-full glass of scotch in front of him. It had been a tense few days.

Something was at the edge of his mind, and he struggled to grasp the words … or was it the emotions that eluded him? *Why am I incapable of expressing my feelings?* When they first met, he sensed more than an ember. Now, it had flamed into a deep passion. *I can admit it to Joseph but can't find the resolve to tell her.*

Out of the corner of his eye, he watched Joseph approach with a beer in his hand.

"Kyle Weston, eating dinner alone. Where are all the women?"

Raking up, Kyle sneered, "Not interested in meaningless sex at the moment."

"That's progress." Joseph took a seat across from him. "Anyone in mind?"

Tipping the glass of scotch to his mouth, he barely nodded.

"Buddy, ya know I love you. And I don't enjoy being pissed at you. I also hate seeing you miserable." Raising his beer bottle, Joseph pointed with it. "Funny, no one knows how to get what he wants better than you. And yet, you've got no life other than work."

Kyle lowered his eyes. "You're right. I don't deserve anything more."

"Kyle, I didn't say that. Wait. When you say more, are you referring to Cate?"

Glimpsing up, he stirred the ice in his drink. Their eyes locked. Joseph sat forward. "Do you really love her?"

"I do. I love her. I have from the beginning. It hurts I love her so much." He slumped in his chair.

"I'm impressed you behaved yourself all these years," his friend extolled.

"She was very young then." Kyle tossed his head. "I actually tried to be with her at the start, and she shot me down ... saying she only wanted to be friends and focus on her career."

"I didn't know. Kyle, you never said anything."

"Frankly, I'm not used to being rejected," he snorted. "Hard on the ego. But it's not about me. I respect what she asked, and I didn't wanna scare her away by pursuing a relationship. It'd kill me to lose her."

Joseph felt a swell of pride for both of them.

"Besides," Kyle noted, "did you forget you threatened me more than once to keep away from her?"

"In the beginning, yes. And yet, after a while, I was impressed by how selfless you were with Cate. Not that way with anyone else ..."

"I'd never hurt Cate," he interrupted. "Never."

"I believe you." Joseph agreed. "Cate turning you down was smart four years ago when you both were younger. As much as I tried to keep you two apart, the reality is everyone knew how much you grew to care for each other. Kyle, she's in love with you. Has been for a long time. You can see it in her eyes when she looks at you."

Kyle's vision flew to Joseph's face. "Really?" For a moment, he felt optimistic, then flashed to memories of so many missed opportunities. "Maybe it's too late. I think I ruined everything."

Staring off in a vague thought, Joseph returned to reality at hearing Kyle's lament. "So, you do love her. I mean, you finally admit you're in love?"

"Hopelessly."

"Remember when you told me there was this marvelous girl you nearly met twice, once at your party? Before I knew it was Cate, I told you it was destiny."

"Well, destiny's shit," Kyle fired back. "It's an endless battle."

"Who're you fighting?"

"Me," he exhaled, chagrined.

"All that's required to discover something or someone who's meant to be is to show up. Destiny takes over." Joseph slapped Kyle on the back. "Stop resisting, Kyle. Tell her you love her. Let destiny work its magic."

Chapter 37
Soul's Journey

As the sky turned a thousand hues of color, the evening was still sweltering. Cate stood alone on the outside patio that rested high on a cliff. The magnificent sunset with a palette of vibrancy filled her with marvel and expectation ... the magic hour.

Inside, there was an atmosphere of celebration at the karaoke establishment, an unofficial wrap party as the end of the Phoenix production loomed closer.

Shepherding the mettle to sing, she entered the air-conditioned restaurant determined to be her character from the film—tenacious, gutsy, and daring ... perhaps after a glass of champagne.

As Joseph and Jessica chatted with some of the crew near the window, she claimed the empty table near the stage.

Kyle was seated alone at the bar. Adrift in thought, replaying Joseph's words, he reflexively peeled the label from his bottle of mineral water. He noticed Cate, their eyes connecting, his heart pounded. This was the moment. Taking a definitive breath, he walked over and kissed her forehead. Then, shockingly, he took the stage. Reticent yet single-minded, he focused on Cate's hypnotic presence.

The music began, one of Van Morrison's intoxicating love songs.

I've been searching a long time for someone exactly like you.

Although the crowd quieted, Kyle sang only to Cate. His eyes never wavered, drawing her into his world.

Someone like you makes it all worthwhile.

She was stunned, captivated. His melodic voice filled her with bliss.

... someone exactly like you.

As the song ended, he slowly stepped off the stage to the wild applause of his colleagues and took a seat close beside Cate.

"You were fantastic," she said, thunderstruck. "That song, the words were astonishing." She paused. "Wait. You don't sing in public. What happened?"

"You did." His mind incited to be bold, he lifted her hand and kissed it, holding it lovingly. "Come with me."

Guiding her past the ruckus, they retreated into the seclusion of the night, leaving the music and chatter trapped behind closed doors.

Outside, the lustrous city glittering below the cliff was a shining carpet of lights. Cate and Kyle were alone in the stillness. A sultry, dry breeze warmed their skin, tossing about their hair as he placed his arm lightly across her shoulder, conquering the awkwardness.

"This is an amazing view," she mused breathlessly. "It's as if the city's a mirror of the heavens."

There was a singular drive in him to embrace her, to kiss her, to caress the curves of her loveliness. Powering his breath, he forced down the inclination.

"I thought you preferred the sun setting on the ocean."

"Yes, they're both splendid ... and different. Why?"

"I bought the house in Malibu, the one you like so much."

"Oh, Kyle." The moonlight reflecting in her eyes only enhanced her awe. "I'm so happy for you!"

"It needs work, renovation. Cate, I want you to help me make it a home ... for both of us."

"Us?" Cate's voice cracked. Bewilderment marred her calm. "Are you asking me to move in? Like a roommate? My mom and brother would have a fit, Kyle. I can't do that." Her heart was racing.

"You misunderstand." He turned her to face him, his look generous and urgent. "I've been hiding, Cate. Trying to avoid making a mistake that would stupidly take you away from me. I'm struggling to find the courage to show you how I feel. We're best friends. And it's paralyzed me."

She let out a soft gasp as he adoringly stroked her cheek.

"When I saw your audition tape, my heart flew to my throat. I've never felt like that ... ever. In truth, I had no idea what love felt like. But with you, it was so immediate, so powerful. Not just a spark ... a crazy bonfire that grew every moment we were together." Fixing upon her angelic face, Kyle's energy seemed to explode. "You're the most extraordinary person I've ever known."

With a kaleidoscope of sensations, barely able to speak, her eyes became misty. "Kyle, it's always been you."

"But you said you wanted time?"

"I did." She gently squeezed his arm. "I didn't mean forever. Just until I got to know you and see if your intentions were ..."

"Honorable?"

"Real," she corrected. "Didn't you get my hints that I was ready to be more than friends?"

"Actually, those *hints* were what confused me. Every time I wanted to be with you ... to make love to you—there were so many times—I'd tell myself not to run off the greatest person in my life ... I was such a fool."

Timidly running her fingers through his hair, Cate unjumbled the flutter of emotions, mesmerized by his gaze.

"No more holding back," he continued, his being now secure, strong. "I love you, Catie. Please love me."

"I do love you." Her eyes still sparkling, she placed her hand on his chest. "Kyle, you're my heart."

Taking her into his arms, he kissed her yearningly.

As the darkening sky veiled the last blush of color, glistening stars illuminated wishes and dreams. Cate and Kyle lingered in their embrace, eyes glowing with an impenetrable bond. A craving that would last a lifetime merged into an overpowering fervor, as if the depths of their souls had collided into one. Savoring every second, time was no longer the enemy but an ally.

From the window, Joseph watched, his smile growing. "I better be the best man."

Chapter 38
Time After Time

The morning light filled the bedroom. Cate woke slowly, Kyle asleep beside her. She rose quietly and stepped into the bathroom to brush her teeth and shower.

Standing at the mirror wrapped in a towel, spreading lotion on her freshly washed skin, she glimpsed Kyle leaning on the door, watching her. She massaged the excess cream onto her hands.

"Good morning," she said.
"Good morning, my beautiful friend."
He briefly considered her, silently smiling.
"What?" She gazed back.
"Marry me?"
She peered at him enchantingly. "Marry you?"
"Absolutely!"
He strolled to stand behind her.
She chuckled. "I *am* married to you, silly. For eighteen years now."
"I married my dream," he said softly.
"We both did."
He laced his arms around her waist, nuzzling her neck. "Mmm, you smell good."

"It's called soap," she brayed.

"No, it's called Cate." He went over to his sink and put toothpaste on his toothbrush. "Did I hear Mia leave?"

"Yeah, she had an early class." Cate went to the bedroom and opened her dresser drawer.

"What's on your agenda today?" she called.

"Nothing until later. Robbie's running the production meeting this morning. What's your schedule?"

"I'm having lunch with Ed and Scott to discuss my new book's contract with Hidden Shelf."

Strolling out of the bathroom, Kyle lay on the bed, propping up the pillow behind his back, again watching her. Standing in her bra and panties, she rummaged in the closet for an outfit to wear to her meeting, carrying her choice over to the corner chair to set it across.

"I had the best dream." He scooted to the center of the bed, readjusting the pillow behind him.

"Another New Orleans' dream?" she joked.

"No, it was about what we discussed before bed last night. What if we met years ago when you first moved to L.A. at eighteen? It wasn't like the New Orleans' one, as vivid as it was. It was more like a movie. I saw the story from everyone's point of view, not just mine."

"So, did we fall in love and live happily ever after?" She set her high heels next to the chair with her outfit.

"Come here, and I'll tell you." He reached out to her.

"Can I get dressed first?"

"No need," he said with a sly smile, "it's only coming off in a few minutes."

She laughed and stepped over. Kyle feistily tugged her hand, coaxing her to lay beside him. He propped a pillow behind her.

"Thank you."

"The dream began sixteen years before we actually met. I was a bit of a rascal."

"And my eighteen or nineteen-year-old self didn't charm you into being a decent guy?"

"Yes, you certainly did." He kissed her lightheartedly.

"I'm curious. What was I like?"

"Infinitely more naïve in a precious way." The memory of the dream brought a naughty glint to his eye.

"I'm shocked we got together." She laid her head on his shoulder. "Okay, my love, tell me the story."

"I'll share the whole dream after I say one thing."

"What?"

Repositioning himself on the bed to sit before her, he ran his fingers through her hair, fondling her head. "I love you, Catie. Turns out, I loved you even before I knew you."

Kyle kissed her gently, their lips yielding. Caressing her beautiful face, he pressed his mouth passionately to hers. Cate's response, as always, enthusiastically matched his intensity.

It would be another *destined* day ...

The End

Future Novels in the Series:

Back to One: Take 5 Hero Shot (2025) will expound on the lives of Cate and Kyle's celebrity children—the overwhelming challenges and treacherous waters they traverse both as individuals and as a strong family unit.

Back to One: Take 6 Persistence of Vision (2026) will be the final novel in the series—when the magic fades.

Follow Antonia Gavrihel and listen to the music included in the *Back to One* Series on BTO's Spotify playlists at:
www.antoniagavrihel.com

On social media:
Instagram and Facebook
@antoniagavrihel

Back to One: Take 5
Hero Shot

Across the room, Kyle lovingly gazed at his wonderful family. Simone walked back to him, standing exceedingly close.

"It's a beautiful place you have here."

"Thank you," Kyle quickly answered, trying to listen to the song.

"Robert tells me you have a fabulous ranch with horses and guest houses. Maybe he'll take me there to visit you sometime."

Kyle side-glanced her, keeping his attention fixed on Cate.

Simone shifted even closer, leaning on him. He glared at her and moved away.

"I wanted to talk to you, Kyle," she said in a confidential voice.

"Maybe later, Simone. I'm trying to watch my family."

"It's been impossible to get you alone all day." She rubbed his arm as sensually as she had rubbed Robbie's at the holiday party.

Pulling away, he again pointed at the singing on the other side of the vast room while hushing her.

"You know, I looked you up. You were quite a player in the day with lots of women. I guess you particularly enjoyed younger women." She simpered with a temptress look.

"Simone, I'm not sure what your point is, but Rob's singing to his niece, and you might want to listen," he scolded.

"I'd rather be alone with you," she cooed.

"What?!" Kyle backed up several steps, quite disgusted.

"Don't run away." She clutched his arm and batted her eyes coyly. "I was simply interested in what a real movie star does in his free time."

"I think you need to get back to Rob," he ordered, yanking his arm from her grasp.

Ignoring his rejection, she waxed seductively. "Your reputation was scandalous once. How exciting! When I think about it, not all that long ago, according to the tabloids," she giggled, referring to the false rumors lobbed by Tracy a few years prior.

His past was still haunting him.

An Exclusive Bonus
Wonderwall – The Movie

The following pages are a sample—the first four scenes—of the complete screenplay of *Wonderwall*, which Cate and Kyle shoot in the novel *Slating Magic Hour*. After the success of *Way Down* in *Ambient Light* and *Dangerous Type* in *Cinéma Vérité*, I wanted to share all the stories they filmed, even early in their careers.

Scan the QR code below for the exclusive free PDF or ebook of the **entire** *Wonderwall* movie script, written in an easy-to-read style.

Gavrihel

WONDERWALL

Cast

Charlie Striker	Kyle Weston
Rose Grady	Bess Allen
Stevie Wyler	Catherine Leigh
Eric Addle	Joseph Beason
Jude Wyler	Ryan Killian
Mike Langston	Eddie Tippler

Screenplay by Davis Whitman

Directed by Ian Parrish

SCENE 1
Nemesis

SCENE: Lobby of a fancy office building. Ron Fueler forces Charlie Striker into the elevator and pushes the top-floor suite. In his late twenties, Charlie is tall, athletic, and handsome. Several inches shorter, Ron is the stereotype of a thug—mean and muscular.

"Action ..."

"Is this really necessary?" Charlie asks with disdain, wrenching his arm from Ron's grasp.
"Mr. Langston has requested your company."
"I have no interest in seeing the bastard." Charlie straightens his jacket and reaches to hit a lower floor button. Ron stops him, revealing a gun beneath his jacket.
"Mr. Langston insists."
"Fine," Charlie snarls. "It's been six years, and that's not long enough. Maybe I'll refresh his memory as to why I hate him."
"Not a good idea unless you want your brains scattered on the floor."
The elevator opens to a vast office suite with only a young woman as the receptionist and an oversized double wooden door leading to a massive private office. She gestures, and they enter.
Mike Langston—late thirties, attractive and muscular—sits behind his giant desk. Langston smokes a cigar and has a glass

of expensive scotch in front of him. He uses a remote to turn down the music. Ron again clutches Charlie's arm, shoves him to the empty chair across from Langston, and treads back to guard the door.

Charlie stares at Langston. "So why am I here?"

Langston takes a long drag from the cigar. The smoke is nauseatingly choking.

"Do you believe in fate, Striker? Well, guess what? In two months, my gallery will exhibit the Imperial Jewels Collection."

"Fate?" Charlie says curtly. "What makes you think I care?"

"I'd imagine you'd want to finish the job this time." Langston fiddles with an access key card. "Rebound from your failure."

"We didn't fail. We were set up, and you know it. We barely got out of there alive."

"Not all of you," smirks Langston.

Charlie sneers, quickly rising, and heads to the door. "Screw you, Langston."

Ron once more shows the gun in his shoulder holster.

As Charlie turns around, Langston blows out a large puff of smoke.

"You were never the brains of the outfit, were you, Striker? Jude Wyler—that was his talent. He'd jump at the chance to redeem himself."

"If he were alive," snaps Charlie.

"Whose fault was that?"

Charlie aggressively crosses to the desk. "It was yours, Langston. Jude was sharp, proficient, and my best friend. That heist, the one you hired us to do, should have never gone wrong."

"Lighten up, Charlie. What would I gain out of you failing?" Langston reclines leisurely in his chair, still toying with his key card.

"What would you get out of us pulling *this* job? It's your gallery hosting the exhibit."

"Let's see, there's insurance money, a slice of the diamonds. Yeah, that'll work for me."

"So, you get the money for insuring the exhibit and still get the loot. Don't you have to give the insurance proceeds to the rightful owner of the gems?"

"I don't care about their insurance. I care about the gallery's losses." He flips the card repeatedly, further annoying Charlie.

"Not interested."

"Striker, you don't have a choice. Does that super genius kid still work in your crew? I heard she graduated college and law school in record time."

"Keep Stevie out of this." Charlie glowers. "She's been through enough."

"How old is she now? Twenty-two?" Langston chuckles.

He narrows his eyes. "Why the interest in Stevie?"

"Maybe she'll come work for me. I can offer her some great benefits." Langston opens his bottle of scotch. "Or the girl might end up with no future at all. That'd be a real shame."

"Leave her alone, Langston," Charlie growls. "I'll discuss it with my crew."

"Of course, Striker." Langston refills his glass of fine scotch. "I can't be involved myself in case of an insurance investigation." He reads from a newspaper he flips open on his desk. "This is all you need to get started. According to the *Arizona Republic,* the exhibit opens in two months with a huge gala for select wealthy socialites the night before the public may attend." He hands the paper to Charlie. "You'll need to learn everything else on your own, understand?"

"Yeah, I get it." Folding the paper, Charlie puts it beneath his arm.

"Oh, Striker, say hi to Stevie for me. I could use a smart beauty on my staff."

Charlie pushes past Ron and slams the door shut.

"And cut."

SCENE 2
Proposal

SCENE: Charlie is having a heated discussion with Eric Addle. About the same age, Eric is nice-looking but a bit lanky. Stephanie "Stevie" Wyler enters loaded with law books, interrupting their conversation. In her early twenties, she is beautiful, petite, and extraordinarily bright.

"Action ..."

"Hey, guys, what's the commotion? I could hear you all the way outside in the street."

"Charlie has a brilliant job for us, except it's impossible, and the guy asking us to do it nearly offed us last time."

"What's Eric talking about, Charlie?" She sets down her books.

"Mike Langston wants us to steal the Imperial Jewels Exhibit when it arrives at the Weatherly Gallery in two months."

"Doesn't he own that gallery?" She stands in front of the two, arms folded.

"Yeah, he does. He'll get the insurance and also expects a cut of the haul." Charlie stares down at the drink in his hand.

"I can't believe you're seriously considering this," Eric spits out venomously, "when he's the son of a bitch who put a hit out on Jude when we tried to rip off the same jewels six years ago."

Stevie says nothing and swiftly walks to her bedroom. Charlie marches to her closed door and tries the knob. It's locked. He taps softly on the door. "Stevie, are you okay?"

No response. Charlie shrugs toward a crestfallen Eric.

"And cut."

SCENE 3
An Odd Sort of Family

SCENE: Flashback to Charlie, Eric, and Jude, Stevie's older brother. The boys are seventeen years old and pumped with adolescent arrogance. Along with being accomplished thieves, they each carry unique talents. Jude is the team's organizer and skilled wheelman, Eric is a programmer and techie, and Charlie is the frontman with charm and personality. Riding in a station wagon, Jude drives them through an exclusive neighborhood. Blind Faith's *Can't Find My Way Home* is playing softly on the radio.

"Action ..."

Eric stares at the back area of the station wagon. Stevie, age eleven, is asleep. "I can't believe you brought your little sister on a job," Eric says quietly to Jude.

Jude glances back, lowering his voice, "I couldn't leave her alone with that crazy woman."

"That's no way to talk about your aunt," Eric chuckles.

"She's not our aunt. Just someone my alcoholic stepfather knew would take us in when he skipped town."

As Jude brings the car to a stop outside an expansive mansion, Eric notes, "Wasn't she better off there than here?"

"Trust me. She's safer with us."

"Are you sure everyone's out of town and the alarm's off?" asks Charlie.

"Absolutely. Tyler said he'd unlock the backdoor," Jude confirms.

"What a jerk. How much is his cut for us ripping off his parents?" Eric flicks a lighter on and off.

"A fourth."

Jude remains in the car as the lookout.

Eric and Charlie put on gloves and creep to the back sliding door. It's locked. They go to the other entries, even the windows. None are unlocked.

"Shit!" Eric muffles his contempt.

Charlie and Eric return to the vehicle.

"What's wrong?" Jude says quietly.

"Tyler screwed us. It's locked solid," says Charlie, angrily sliding into the passenger seat. "Let's go!"

"No, I need this money," Jude demands. "I've got to take care of my sister and get our own place."

"Well, I spotted a tiny window in the kitchen cracked open," Eric says from the backseat. "But none of us can fit through it."

Jude peeks at his sleeping sister. "Stevie can do it."

Jude gently shakes the youngster's arm. "Stevie, wake up ... we've got a job for you."

Moments later, Jude lifts his sister, and she climbs in the window, sporting an extra pair of Charlie's large gloves. Moving carefully to the back door, she unlatches it.

The station wagon speeds down the road, Van Morrison's *Wild Nights* playing loudly on the radio. The four outlaws are hooting, laughing, and celebrating the considerable haul.

"This settles it," Charlie says at the top of his voice. "We're now a four-member team. Stevie, you're awesome!"

A montage plays out as the years pass. They've become invincible thieves, executing virtually impossible burglaries and heists, always invisible to law enforcement, and getting a reputation in the underworld as the best in the business. They could slide into any structure in numerous undetectable ways, from picking complex locks to slinking through tight crawl spaces. Once, Stevie scaled a five-story warehouse to get into an open window, Eric shakily following her.

Stevie also becomes an able wheelman, having learned evasive driving maneuvers from her brother. The four have formed not only a crack team of thieves but a family, residing together in a large four-bedroom house.

Their life is nearly idyllic … and the competition is growing resentful of their adeptness.

"And cut."

SCENE 4
Presaging

SCENE: Flashback continues to high school graduation. Stevie—only sixteen years old—is the class valedictorian. Watching her on stage, Jude, Charlie, and Eric proudly sit in the front row of the parents' section, mesmerized as she concludes her poignant speech.

"Action ..."

Jude hugs Stevie. "I'm so proud of you. I can't believe you made it through high school this quickly."

Eric hikes up to Jude and nods. Sighing, Jude offers, "We have a little business tonight. Have fun at the graduation dance. Here are the keys to the station wagon. We'll use the van. I'll see you in the morning."

"Jude, the Emery Museum? Can't you do it tomorrow instead?" Stevie pleads, "Let's go out and celebrate my graduation. All of us, please?"

"No, the museum's closing early tonight to prepare for tomorrow's fundraiser. It's our best chance."

"Then I'll go with you," offers Stevie anxiously.

"No, kiddo. Have fun at your graduation party." Jude gazes at his sister with affection.

"But what if you need me?"

"This one's a piece of cake." Jude winks.

"Jude, please," Stevie begs. "I have a bad feeling about this."

"Stop fretting," he laughs and taps her forehead. "It'll give you wrinkles, brainiac!" He kisses her head, and the three depart.

As the DJ plays Duran Duran's *Save a Prayer*, a handsome graduate comes to flirt with Stevie. In her mind, she imagines his friends laughing and jeering that he is speaking to her. Young, awkward, and a bit of a geek, she shies away from the boy, standing off to the side. Her thoughts are preoccupied with the job she should be on.

Finally, Stevie has had enough. She jumps into the station wagon and speeds to the museum. She slams on the brakes, gasping. There are police everywhere. She desperately scans the area. The van is nowhere to be found. Panicking, she focuses her disturbed thoughts ... the rendezvous point. Making a U-turn, she heads to it and spots the van parked off the road under a viaduct. Leaping out of the car and hurrying over, she slides open the side door, causing Charlie to draw his weapon.

"Stevie, no!" Charlie frantically warns.

Too late. Stevie sees Jude lying on the van floor, Eric crying, blood everywhere.

"Jude!" she screams.

He looks up weakly. "Hey, kiddo. Guess it wasn't as easy as I imagined."

"Why aren't we on the way to a hospital," she shouts at Eric and Charlie.

Eric shakes his head. Charlie, whose right arm is in a makeshift tourniquet from also being shot, gently puts his hand on her shoulder. "There's nothing we can do, Stevie," he whispers, tears flowing from his eyes. "The wounds are fatal."

Hysterically crying, Stevie holds Jude in her arms. "Do something," she hollers at Eric.

"Kiddo, it's okay," comforts Jude. "Don't worry about me. I'll be with Mom soon." He grips the St. Jude medal around his neck. "Stevie, wear this for protection. It'll keep you safe."

"Didn't work tonight, did it?" she cries scornfully, her face drenched with tears.

"Yeah, it did. It kept you out of harm's way. That's all that matters." He tries to inhale, wincing from the pain.

"No, Jude, you can't leave me alone!"

"I won't." He glances up at Charlie and Eric. "Guys, take care of my little sister. Swear to me."

"We will," Eric weeps.

"Always." Charlie can barely speak.

"Stevie, promise me, you'll make something of yourself. Not this crap job. You're smarter than me. I love you ..."

"Jude, don't go ... I love you too."

The three are silent—their team forever one man down.

Back to the present, Stevie stares at the St. Jude medal hanging from her neck, memories of her brother's death six years ago haunting her. She exits her room to observe Eric and Charlie in the kitchen.

"We'll do it," she states emphatically, "but we're not giving Langston a damn thing. And for what he did to Jude, we'll do the job so he gets busted for the theft. He's going down!"

"And cut."

About the Author
Antonia Gavrihel

Born to an entertainment family—her mother a big band singer, and father a comedian and actor—Antonia grew up accompanying her parents to soundstages, movie sets, and recording studios. During these formative years, she began her own acting career. Although she enjoyed this creative outlet, her constant companion was the written word. The dream of being an author inspired Antonia. Drawn to the freedom writing offered and imagination made present on paper, she won an honorable mention in a national poetry contest at the age of twelve.

In the 1990s, Antonia crafted a story about a perfect friendship, *Back to One*. After a year of writing into the wee hours of the morning, she began submitting her first complex manuscript to various publishers … for the next twenty-five years. Persistence is one of the main lessons of both the entertainment and writing life. In 2020, she established a flourishing association with Hidden Shelf Publishing House.

Slating Magic Hour is Antonia's fourth novel in the award-winning series.

Back to One (2021) introduced the readers to relatable, engaging characters and was met with immediate success, rave reviews, and accolades.

Ambient Light (2022), the second in the series, revealed Cate and Kyle's connection deepening.

Cinéma Vérité (2023) exposed the darker side of celebrity.

With a unique addition to her novels, she has given readers bonus playscripts—*Way Down* with *Ambient Light*, *Dangerous Type* with *Cinéma Vérité*, and *Wonderwall* with *Slating Magic Hour*.

Made in the USA
Columbia, SC
16 March 2025